CONFRONTING THE INVISIBLE

Carlyle & West Mysteries
Book Three

David Field

Also in the Carlyle & West Mystery Series
Interviewing the Dead
Death Comes But Twice
Death Among The Nightingales

CONFRONTING THE INVISIBLE

Published by Sapere Books.

20 Windermere Drive, Leeds, England, LS17 7UZ,
United Kingdom

saperebooks.com

ISBN: 978-1-80055-117-6

1

Matthew West, his fiancée Adelaide Carlyle, and her father James Carlyle were enjoying a pot of tea in the sitting room on the first floor of the Carlyle house in Victoria Park Road, Hackney. Matthew was looking down in some curiosity at the procession of gaily painted wagons, converted horse buses and large flat conveyances full of wild animals in cages that were clomping and rattling their way down the road beyond the front gate.

'It's Baxter's Circus,' Carlyle told him.

'A circus?' Matthew echoed.

Adelaide nodded. 'I used to get so excited when I was a small girl and we saw them arriving. Now I'm afraid it holds less romance for me.'

'Hardly surprising,' her father commented. 'You've seen the more sordid side of life for these people. During their performances they're all spangle and glitter, but afterwards they're nursing sores, scabs, and the other side-effects of a rough life on the road without adequate food or sanitation.'

'Father's their unofficial physician,' Adelaide explained. 'He began attending on them some years ago, when we were watching an afternoon performance and one of the clowns broke his arm. Father set it for him, only to find himself with a queue of performers suffering from God knows what. Since then, every year he regards it as his duty to look in on them and see what he can do for them.'

'These days I take Adelaide with me,' Carlyle added, 'given her determination to become the nurse of every child in the nation. The parents don't always thank her for advising them that their offspring are undernourished, but she still does it.'

'It's hardly surprising that the children fall prey to infections,' Adelaide replied with distaste written all over her face, 'given the total lack of hygiene and the exposure to animal dung and suchlike. I don't suppose this year will be any different.'

'You still continue to act as their unofficial doctor?' Matthew asked Carlyle.

'Yes. Free of charge, what's more. But I doubt that anyone else would undertake the task, and I have no need of the money. They'll be here in Victoria Park for at least two weeks, to judge by previous years, and they'll set up on that flat ground just inside the Queen's Gate.'

'I assume that they have their own circuit of places to visit at the same time every year,' Matthew commented, 'but what do they do during the winter months?'

'As far as I know, they have a place somewhere in Surrey to which they retreat once the weather closes in,' Adelaide told him. 'That's what some of their children told me when I enquired about their schooling. So the poor mites only get half the education that they need, although most of them are being trained up to work in the circus anyway.'

'It must be every child's dream to be travelling with a circus,' Matthew said. 'When I was little, Charles, Caroline and myself were always taken to see "Bentley's Menagerie and Travelling Show" when it set up in Lincoln's Inn Fields. I always imagined myself as one of the boys leading an elephant around the ring, while Charles saw himself as a high-wire artist, and Caroline loved the clowns.'

'Very romantic, I'm sure,' Adelaide sniffed, 'but from what I can see for myself, those children are being used like servants

— slaves, even. It's high time that the authorities stepped in, like they did with the poor chimney sweeps.'

'Something you can perhaps campaign for when you next stand for the London County Council,' Matthew suggested. 'And perhaps I could be of assistance in that, by pointing out that their travelling lifestyle probably means that they have no opportunity for regular church attendance, thereby placing their souls at peril.'

'I'm more concerned for their bodily health and welfare — not to mention their lack of education, and their exploitation,' Adelaide replied. 'But I suppose I'll have to get used to thinking like a curate's wife.'

Adelaide and Matthew were due to be married in two months' time, on Saturday 14th of October, in the parish church of St Dunstan's, Stepney, of which Matthew was now the curate following his return to the Anglican mainstream after five years as a Wesleyan street preacher.

Matthew regarded it as a minor miracle that Adelaide had agreed to marry him, given her background as the only daughter of a fiery Ulster mother whose literary ambitions had been thwarted by the male establishment. Adelaide had grown up in her mother's image, but without her social restraint. For Adelaide and her coterie of like-minded young women, the male bastions of professional life were to be stormed. Not that they stooped to violence, or even public disorder — they left that to the more radical 'Suffragists' and their recently emerged offshoot the 'Suffragettes'. Their approach was less strident, but no less determined, and their ultimate goal was the public recognition of the equality of women in all aspects of political and professional life. This clearly provided a challenge to anyone seeking to interest Adelaide in the more mundane role of wife and mother, which would bind her to the home and nursery, and limit her ability to excel in her professional life, but somehow — and to his gratified astonishment — Matthew seemed to have won Adelaide's heart.

'Do you still retain an interest in the circus?' Carlyle enquired of Matthew. 'My reason for asking is that when Adelaide and I call on them in a medical capacity, although we don't get paid for our services, we're always given free tickets. You could come over for an early supper one evening, and we could then make up a little party and savour the thrill of the big top. We always get ringside seats, and you could stay overnight with us afterwards.'

Three nights later, Matthew took up Carlyle's generous offer, and the three of them sat ringside as the traditional opening parade of exotic animals marched around the ring. Matthew held his breath while the lion tamer kept a fierce, wild-maned lion at bay with a whip and a stool, and laughed at the tumbling of the clowns as they distracted the audience while circus hands climbed the supporting poles under the giant canvas, fixing trapezes and other exotic devices from the crossbars.

Then there was a roll of drums from the four-piece band to the side of the main ring as the Ringmaster stepped back into the centre of the sawdust, placed the megaphone to his lips and announced, 'Ladies and Gentlemen, to delight, fascinate and terrify you, please welcome — all the way from Italy — the death-defying, the gravity-defeating, the heart-pounding "Incredible Flying Rossi Family!"'

There was a flurry of sparkles as into the circle of light cast by the naphthalene flares ran a mixed group of five, all wearing the same gold leggings and bright red and green tunics. There were two men, two middle-aged women and a younger woman who was clearly intended to be the 'glamour' of the act as she sashayed, swirled and cavorted around the ring, then with a wave of each hand commanded the two men to climb up the two ropes that each gave access to a trapeze hanging perilously from the centre of the big top. They remained there once they'd completed their climb, while the two older women jumped high off the sawdust to claim a lower hanging trapeze each, then execute a series of seemingly impossible contortions as they hung, swung and dangled.

The applause from the appreciative audience had barely died down before the Ringmaster was back in the centre with his megaphone. 'Giuseppe and Roberto will now court death yet again with their amazing, and seemingly impossible, mid-air switch,' he announced. 'Please note the absence of any safety net, so you might wish to duck if they miss their connection.'

Another roll on the drums accompanied the first of the two men — the one on the right as Matthew, Adelaide and James were looking up at them — as he swung upwards on his trapeze for long enough to hook his feet into the crossbar and hang down like a bat in a cave with his arms extended in front of him. The man to the left then extended both arms in a wide and melodramatic gesture as he balanced on the bar of the trapeze, then fell forward in a death dive towards the ground that forced screams from the mouths of the audience before they realised that his extended hands were about to be caught by the man on the right hanging by his feet.

Their hands touched and closed on each other, and then — seemingly in slow motion to those who watched on in horror — the falling man gave a shriek of fear as his hands slipped from the rescuing grasp and he fell, head-first, into the sawdust.

The women on the lower trapezes screamed, and the younger girl stopped her cavorting and ran forward to throw herself on the prone form, shrieking loudly.

There was pandemonium in the audience as those with young children rose from their seats and made for the exit. All around could be heard screams, shouts of disbelief and strident cries of horror, as Carlyle turned to Adelaide and instructed her to accompany him into the centre of the ring. He leaned down over the inert form, hissed, 'Broken neck, clearly,' for Adelaide's benefit, then just to make sure he took hold of the dead man's wrist with a view to testing his pulse. He withdrew his hand with a puzzled expression, looked down at it, and gave Adelaide a further instruction. 'Open my medical bag and give me a spatula and one of those empty glass phials. Quickly!'

Adelaide did as requested, and her father scraped something from the dead man's palm, and transferred it to the phial. He repeated the process several times, then sealed the phial and handed it to Adelaide with instructions to put it in his bag. Carlyle called to Matthew, 'Am I correct in recalling that there was a uniformed bobby outside the tent when we came in?'

'That's right, there was,' Matthew confirmed. 'I think he was there to preserve order among the crowd that was queuing to get in, most of whom now seem to be fighting to get out.'

'Go and find him, then ask him to go to whatever police office he's attached to, and have this body conveyed down to the hospital in a wagon, for me to examine first thing tomorrow. Unless I'm very much mistaken, this man was murdered.'

2

'I came as soon as I got your message at the Yard,' Inspector John Jennings told Carlyle and Adelaide once they answered his knock on the mortuary door, 'but I have to record the fact that I have yet to have breakfast, and that my caseload is such that I have better things to investigate than the accidental death of a travelling mountebank.'

'It wasn't accidental,' Carlyle assured him. 'We have every reason for believing that he was murdered.' He recounted the events they had witnessed the previous evening. 'The man dived off a trapeze high up in the big top, clearly of the belief that the man who was dangling by his feet from another trapeze a few feet away would catch him as he plummeted towards the ground. It seems that this was the climax of their regular show, and logic suggests that it had never failed before. But this time, very clearly to my eyes anyway, while the two touched hands, and appeared to make the necessary connection, the victim then seemed to slip from the catcher's grasp, and broke his neck when he hit the sawdust twenty feet below.'

'So cause of death was nothing more sinister than sweaty palms?' Jennings concluded with a frown.

'No,' Carlyle continued. 'While checking his wrist pulse to confirm "life extinct", I encountered something moist on the dead man's palm. It certainly wasn't simply perspiration, and I brought a sample back here to the laboratory, along with the body. Adelaide conducted the necessary analysis and she can take over from here.'

'It's some crude form of grease,' Adelaide told Jennings, 'and to judge by the smell, it's basic cooking lard. If you've ever slipped on any in your kitchen at home, you'll know that it's very greasy to the touch.'

'My wife has higher hygiene standards than that,' Jennings muttered. 'But as I understand it, you're trying to tell me that for some reason the dear departed had smeared his palms with cooking oil, knowing that this would prevent the other man being able to catch him. Doesn't that make it either suicide or an attempt to bring a civil action for negligence against the circus?'

Carlyle fixed Jennings with an irritated stare. 'I realise that you would much prefer to be somewhere else, but there's no need to be so obtuse, Inspector. My suggestion is that the lard came from the hand of the man who was supposed to catch him, which makes it murder.'

'What's this man's name, and where will I find him?'

'I've no idea of the man's name,' Carlyle admitted, 'but no doubt the circus people can tell you. He was part of a family act calling itself "The Flying Rossis", or something like that, and the circus will still be pitched just inside Victoria Park in Hackney. They'll probably cancel this evening's show as a mark of respect, but last night was only the third night of what was meant to be a fortnight of performances.'

'So you want me to go questioning a man who may have murdered another by means of greasy hands, eight hours after he may be presumed to have cleaned up the evidence, is that it?' Jennings asked.

'If you can discover a motive, and with the evidence of the lard on the victim's hands, can't you even make out enough of a case to have the man arrested, and then seek to get a confession out of him?' Adelaide asked.

Jennings gave a hollow laugh. 'You've obviously joined that growing section of the local community who believe that we acquire confessions by beating suspects with billy clubs. I can just imagine the questions put to me by Defence Counsel at any trial, such as "You never found any of this hypothetical grease on my client's hand, did you?" or "Are you seriously asking the jury to believe that my client managed to climb a rope, then perform several intricate manoeuvres on a trapeze twenty feet above the ground, while his hands were smeared with lard?"'

'You're just going to give up then, are you?' Carlyle demanded with an edge to his voice.

'No, because you can't give up something that you never started in the first place. I can't waste police time on a hopeless case when I've just buckled someone we've been after for months.'

'Someone more important than a murderer?' Carlyle challenged.

Jennings nodded with a smirk of pride. 'Infinitely. Someone who's been getting up the noses of the genteel but poverty stricken ladies of the better districts of this city. This very clever fraudster placed advertisements in the "Personal" columns of newspapers circulating in the area, claiming to be the "Marquis of Glengarry", who of course doesn't exist. He further claimed to be looking for a housekeeper for his London residence, and the unsuspecting dupes who answered, no doubt hoping to find a suitable position with a titled employer, found themselves hosting — in their own sitting rooms, mind you — this plausible middle-aged gent who filled their heads with stories of receptions and balls during the season, summers spent grouse shooting in the Highlands, yachting trips out of Cowes, you name it. There were also subtle hints that, as a widower, he might be in the market for future matrimony.'

'Then he seduced them?' Adelaide asked with a grimace.

Jennings shook his head. 'Nothing so crude. He advised each of the ladies that they would, naturally, be required to present the right appearance for his house guests, and asked to see what items of jewellery they possessed. They duly produced their pathetic trinkets, and our pretend Marquis then gave each lady a cheque with which to acquire more appropriate items of jewellery. He then made some excuse that caused them to leave their sitting rooms again, such as a request for another cup of tea or whatever, and in their absence snaffled the jewellery and made a hasty exit. Every item we know about finished up in a local pawn shop, and needless to say the cheques bounced when presented.'

'Very slippery,' Carlyle agreed. 'So how did you catch him?'

'We had a few photographs of previous fraudsters of our acquaintance, and very soon our evasive Marquis had been identified as Edmund "Neddy" Smith, so we had him followed. We nabbed him in the act of pawning the latest jewels, and seven women so far have come forward and identified him.'

'Well done,' Adelaide said. 'It's bad enough that some women of gentle birth and good breeding are obliged by circumstances to be seeking such menial and degrading positions in the households of men, without their being preyed on.'

'You've clearly satisfied my daughter that your somewhat skewed sense of priorities can be justified,' Carlyle frowned, 'but I still believe that this case of mine deserves some attention.'

'Then do it yourself,' Jennings suggested as he eased himself off the stool on which he'd been perched, and headed for the door.

'We surely can't leave it at that?' Adelaide said once Jennings had left.

Her father shrugged. 'I can't devote any time to further enquiries, even if I knew how to begin.'

'But a man's died — murdered!' Adelaide protested. 'He may have had a wife and children — we *must* do something, surely?'

'If you feel so deeply about it, then go ahead,' Carlyle invited her.

Adelaide screwed up her face. 'I can't just wander in there on my own without a good excuse. The only one I can think of is the usual one of checking on the health of the children, but you normally come with me on those occasions. Will you come with me this time?'

'I'm far too busy, my dear,' Carlyle objected. 'And Jennings may have had a valid point — these people are wandering circus types, here today and gone tomorrow. I have dead bodies of former fulltime London residents awaiting my scalpel, and what I suspect is a Scarlatina outbreak to deal with. If you don't want to go on your own, why not take Matthew? I seem to recall that he was hoping to spread the Gospel among the travelling folk.'

'I can't believe that Jennings refused to do anything, after what you've told me,' Matthew responded when Adelaide presented herself at St Dunstan's without notice, 'but any chance to be with you rather than listening to Mrs Dalby rambling on about the hymn book duty roster is something that I'll gratefully accept.'

'I have the coach waiting outside, if you're free for an hour or two,' Adelaide said. 'I thought we might return to the circus and see what else we can discover that might light a fuse under Jennings. But when we get there, we mustn't say anything about our suspicion that the man may have been murdered. You'll be there to bring spiritual comfort to the bereaved, while I'll be there to check on the health of the circus children. Agreed?'

Matthew happily agreed, and by late morning they were walking down the dusty grass towards the big top. As they got closer, a large man with close-cropped grey hair emerged from under the entrance arch and walked towards them with a big smile. 'That's Edgar Baxter, part-owner and Ringmaster,' Adelaide told Matthew. 'You might not have recognised him without his hat and megaphone. Remember — not a word about murder.'

'Miss Carlyle, what a surprise and a pleasure!' Baxter oozed as he held out a fleshy paw, took Adelaide's gloved hand and kissed it. 'And who, may I ask, is your lucky companion?'

'My fiancé, and the curate of St Dunstan's in Stepney. He was here with my father and I the other evening, and witnessed the — the…'

'Yes indeed — most tragic,' Baxter minced unconvincingly. 'Is that the reason for your welcome return today?'

'Yes and no,' Adelaide said. 'I have yet to set up my annual visiting clinic, although my father unfortunately cannot be in attendance with me on this occasion. But the Reverend West here thought that he might be able to bring some words of comfort to the bereaved, since I believe that the man who died so tragically was part of a family act.'

'Yes indeed — the Rossi family, now sadly missing their star turn. The man who died was the only one who wasn't family, but he was regarded as an honorary Rossi, if you see what I mean. His real name was "Roberto Mancini", but we knew him by his Anglicised name of "Robert Manston", under which he travelled from Italy as part of the act only earlier this year. His was the best English in the entire troupe, who were enjoying their first season here in Hackney. They're currently combining their mourning with the creation of an altogether new act. We aim to start up the shows again with tomorrow's matinee performance.'

'So the others don't speak much English?' Matthew asked. 'I recall speaking to the young girl who was part of their act on the fatal night, and she seemed to prefer to speak in what I assume, from what you tell me, must have been Italian.'

'That would have been Luciana, or "Lucy" as we call her. She's the daughter of the troupe leader Giuseppe — or "George" — Rossi. The remainder of the original troupe are George's wife Tarsia, and his sister Anna. They all speak a smattering of English, but it was George who did all their talking for them.'

'Did?' Adelaide queried.

Baxter nodded. 'Yes — we haven't seen him since the night of the tragedy. He's probably taken himself off to some local Catholic church or other to pray for forgiveness for his clumsiness in failing to catch poor old Robert properly. The women aren't sure whether or not he'll want to go back into the air, so they're practising a routine just between themselves. They'd hoped to stage a finale in which they threw Lucy from one trapeze to another, but at present she's not very well — probably still suffering from the shock of it all.'

'Perhaps we'd better see them first,' Adelaide suggested as she took up the valuable cue.

Matthew nodded sagely. 'I'm Anglican, not Catholic, but even so I can give them some consoling words from the Bible. Although of course it'll be in English.'

'Please feel free,' Baxter invited them. 'You'll find them in the open space behind their travelling wagon, just over there on your right.'

Five minutes later Adelaide and Matthew had joined the three women, who moved to sit on the grass as they gave up the seats on the wagon steps to their visitors. Matthew smiled at the young woman he remembered from two nights previously, and asked her how she was feeling. She hesitated for a moment, perhaps while finding the appropriate words in a language that was not hers, then replied, 'I am being desolate.'

'Luciana, she do nothing but crying,' one of the older woman told them both. 'I am her mama, but she listens not when I say all must pass one day. Instead, she cry, she fall on ground, she not eat.'

'You must be Tarsia, is that correct?' Adelaide asked.

The woman nodded. 'Tarsia Rossi, that is me. You come find Giuseppe?'

'No, we were told that he was missing, perhaps praying in a church nearby,' Matthew told her, and to his amazement she turned her head and spat on the grass.

'Giuseppe, he pray only to the money. Always the money. And he promise to beat poor Luciana when she too sick to climb the ropes when she get the whirly head.'

'You suffer from dizziness?' Adelaide asked as she looked meaningfully at Luciana, who dropped her gaze and nodded, almost in shame.

'Yes. Much when in air, but also when rise from bed.'

'And you are not eating?' was Adelaide's next question as a thought came to her.

Luciana shook her head. 'I am being sick.'

'Best not ask more,' chimed in the second woman. 'She is much in *tristezza — qual è la parola*?' she asked of the first woman, who nodded and translated for Adelaide's benefit.

'She say "sadness". But she right — not to ask more.'

'Have any of the rest of you suffered this sickness and dizziness?' Adelaide asked. The two older women shook their heads. 'So it's not some infection,' Adelaide muttered to Matthew from the corner of her mouth, then turned to address the other woman, who she took to be the aunt. 'How long has Luciana been sick?' she asked.

It was the mother who replied. 'It start in Norwich — six weeks. Giuseppe he say she not really ill.'

'Luciana must eat only dry food — bread, toast and so on,' Adelaide said. 'And she must drink plenty of liquid, but not the water that you find in the river, or even in the taps here. You understand?'

'Yes,' Tarsia replied. 'She is *incinta*, perhaps? It was that way with me.' Tarsia raised her hands over her stomach in an indication of swelling.

'Perhaps,' Adelaide nodded. 'She must not go back into the act, if so.'

'I need to set up my clinic, just in case there are children with a similar affliction to Luciana's,' Adelaide told Matthew as they walked away from the Rossi family group.

'I sincerely hope not,' Matthew replied. 'I don't speak Italian, but even I worked out that Luciana's in the family way. And some family! The father runs off after murdering his partner in the act, and from what I could gather he cared only for money, and was still insisting that his own daughter risk not only her own health, but that of her unborn child, by continuing to contribute to the family trapeze act. In all the circumstances I think it highly unlikely that he's in some church somewhere, praying for absolution.'

'I have to agree with you,' Adelaide replied, 'but it does raise two interesting questions in my mind. The first is whether or not he actually knew that Luciana's pregnant, and the second is whether or not he's run away because he murdered Roberto. Anyway, stay with me while I begin examining a few of the circus children, since it'll give you an idea of what I intend to do for the children in your Bible Class once I'm Mrs West.'

'I was hoping you'd start well before then,' Matthew said. 'But perhaps some of these circus children would also like to learn the story of Jesus.' He caught the look on her face and smiled as he added, 'I know — "Don't push your luck".'

It was well after the customary dinner hour before Adelaide had finished examining the dozen or so children who formed a line in front of her table and chair while she examined them for headlice, enquired about their eating habits and warned one or two of them that they were too overweight to be healthy. As the last of the children was opening her mouth under Adelaide's gentle instruction, Matthew was conscious of Luciana peering enquiringly round the side of the main tent. He walked over to her with a broad smile, and enquired, in the simplest English he could muster, whether or not she wished to be examined by Adelaide. She shook her head, then to his amazement took his hand and placed it on her head.

'My baby. You will bless?' she asked, pointing down towards her stomach.

Matthew duly obliged with a Protestant blessing in English, which probably meant little to Luciana. Then it occurred to him that there might be a horrible reason why the girl felt that she needed some sort of spiritual cleansing, so he gently asked, 'The father?'

Luciana's face crumpled with tears as she whispered her response, and Matthew nodded his understanding and gave her another blessing before she slipped away in further floods of tears.

He walked over to where Adelaide was putting a few basic implements back into her bag. 'I think I just found the motive for why George Rossi arranged the death of his theatrical partner Roberto,' he told her. 'Luciana wanted to see me for some sort of blessing bordering upon absolution for her sin.'

'What sin — getting herself pregnant, you mean?'

'Yes, precisely that. But the father was Roberto Mancini.'

3

Matthew tried his best to keep the frustration from his face as he strove yet again to get across to the children in his Junior Bible Class the miracle of the Resurrection. He made every allowance for the fact that the half dozen or so of them who regularly presented themselves on Thursday afternoons, after they'd returned from the various board schools that they attended, were working-class, and that therefore their only encounter with death would be likely to have been sudden and brutal, but even so he was struggling.

The main difficulty, so far as he could deduce, was that none of them were prepared to contemplate the possibility of a miracle happening, even in another part of the world almost two thousand years ago. Their lives were confined within the harsh reality of fathers struggling to bring home enough money for the family — usually a large one — to eat for another week once the rent was paid, mothers constantly hanging up grey washing above the meagre fire in the corner of an all-purpose room, and noisy arguments in the alleyways by which their single-room dwellings were surrounded that often as not resulted in sudden and violent death.

How could such children be expected to even comprehend, never mind accept, that there was once a man who led his life in such an exemplary fashion that when he died God allowed him to return to give further inspiration and instruction to the Disciples that he'd left behind, mourning his passing?

In the end, Matthew gave up the challenge. 'Let's just forget specific miracles for a moment, and talk about the general idea,' he finally suggested.

Tommy Tideswell asked, 'What's "specific" mean, sir?'

'It means particular, or individual. For example, if you have a bag of apples, and I ask you to give me one from the bag, then the one you give me would be the "specific" one. Does that help?'

'Never 'ad a 'ole bag've apples, sir,' Sammy Thresher complained, while the response of Clarrie Hopgood, the only girl in the group, was, 'I wouldn't give it ter yer, even if I 'ad a bag full've 'em, neither.'

'Well, let's try another example,' Matthew responded, ever the optimist. 'Clarrie, do you have brothers and sisters?'

'Just two bruvvers,' she replied.

Matthew seized the opportunity. 'So you're the only "specific" child in your family who's a girl, aren't you?'

'Does that mean kinda special?' she asked hopefully.

Matthew nodded. 'Exactly. You're very special to your parents, because you're the only "specific" child who's a girl.'

'Does that mean that me mam an' dad don't give a farvin' fer me, 'cos I'm one o' five boys?' Sammy asked, looking crestfallen.

Matthew hastened to correct any wrong impression he might have given. 'No, Sammy, that's *not* what I meant. Every child is special to their parents, because they love them. You've got very fair hair — do your brothers have the same as you?'

'Not really,' Sammy conceded. 'The rest is kinda mucky brown, if yer get me.'

'So you're the specific boy in your family with fair hair, see?' Matthew asked, and Sammy nodded.

'An' that lady what's waitin' fer yer outside's "spersifik" ter you, ain't she?' asked Tommy, who'd been staring out of the window while this exchange had been taking place.

Matthew followed his gaze, and saw Adelaide standing in front of a gravestone in the churchyard, reading its inscription while she waited for Matthew's class to finish, so that they could begin to take measurements inside the newly completed Curate's House with a view to selecting furnishings ahead of their wedding in October.

'Indeed she is,' Matthew confirmed with a smile. 'She's going to become my wife in a few months' time — would you all like to meet her?'

A chorus of eager affirmatives followed this offer, and Matthew walked outside to where Adelaide was standing, then led her by the hand back inside the church hall and got her to stand next to him at the front.

'This is Miss Adelaide, and after October you'll know her as Mrs West, the curate's wife,' Matthew announced proudly. 'She's the daughter of a doctor, so if any of you are feeling sick, she'll be able to help. She'll be living with me in the new house that's just been finished on the other side of the churchyard.'

'Hello, all of you,' Adelaide replied confidently. 'I hope to get to know you all once I settle in, but there's no reason why this little group can't meet me first. What has Matthew — the Reverend West, that is — been teaching you?'

'That we's all special,' Sammy chimed up.

Adelaide smiled kindly at him. 'Indeed you are. To your parents — and to God, if you behave yourselves. Every child is a gift from God.'

Matthew stared in amazed admiration at this sudden display of religious sentiment in his bride-to-be, who when they met had been a virtual atheist, such had been her dreadful experience of the Church in her formative years. Then he was brought back down to earth by a rare contribution from Billy Crabbe.

'Every sprog up ah alley's a gift from me dad — or leastways, that's what me mam sez.'

'He must be a very caring man,' Adelaide replied diplomatically, suppressing the urge to giggle, and Matthew decided that the time had come to end the class.

'Miss Adelaide and I have to go and look over our new house,' he announced, 'so we'll make that the end of Bible Class for today. See you all next Thursday at four o'clock sharp. And if you'd like to bring a friend along with you, that will be fine.'

The children needed no further invitation, and the scraping back of chairs was followed by the collective pounding of boots as the class dispersed into the late afternoon sunlight of that clear spring day.

'Did I pass the test?' Adelaide asked smilingly.

Matthew shrugged. 'We'll wait and see how many references there are to you during next week's class. That's usually a good indication of what they've absorbed from the previous week.'

'There aren't many children here, are there?' Adelaide asked.

'Only seven. I'm hoping it'll grow over time.'

As they walked out of the church hall, Matthew became aware of a well-dressed lady holding Tommy Tideswell firmly by the arm and shouting at him. Tommy was squirming hard in an obvious attempt to make good his escape, but the lady was having none of it.

'You and he were often larking about together behind my back, and contrary to my instructions, so you *must* know something, and you're going to stay right there until the curate here gets you to admit it!' the woman insisted as she turned towards Matthew and Adelaide with an implied request for assistance.

'What seems to be the trouble?' Matthew asked in his best ecclesiastical voice.

The lady snorted indignantly. 'It's this little boy,' she complained. 'My Edgar didn't come home for his tea yesterday, and he's not been home since. His father insists that it's just boys' games, but this little devil was always enticing him away from his duties and responsibilities, and I've no doubt that he knows where the boy's gone, and what he's been up to.'

Matthew treated Tommy to a stern look as he asked, 'And do you, Tommy?'

'No, sir — 'onest ah don't!' the boy insisted.

Matthew tried another approach. 'Can you tell us where Edgar best liked to play?'

'Down the river, else along the canal cut down Lime'ouse way,' Tommy replied.

Mrs Holroyd grabbed his ear and began to pull hard. 'Thanks to the bad habits that *you* taught him, you little beggar!' she shouted.

'Mrs Holroyd, please let go,' Matthew requested sternly.

As she did so Tommy wriggled free, only to be caught by Adelaide, who examined his ear before glaring accusingly at Mrs Holroyd. 'One of your rings cut his ear.'

'No more than he deserves, scruffy urchin that he is,' was the lady's response. 'And who might you be?' she asked by way of afterthought.

'She's my fiancée,' Matthew told her before Adelaide could fire back. 'Miss Adelaide Carlyle, a doctor's daughter who'll be attending, free of charge, to any illnesses that the parish children may have when she becomes my wife.'

'She can start with the nits,' Mrs Holroyd replied huffily. 'Every one of those dreadful children in your Bible Class has nits, and there's no way that any child of mine will be attending while that state of affairs continues.'

'I take it she was referring to headlice?' Matthew asked when Mrs Holroyd had marched off.

Adelaide nodded. 'There can't be a child from a working-class home around here that doesn't have them. I'll come along to your next class, and if you get them to sit down for me I'll get rid of their little parasite problem. I'll also check you over, just in case you got too close to one of your little converts.'

The following week, Adelaide turned up with a small medical bag that was one of her father's cast-offs, and before Matthew began the formal class, he introduced her.

'I think you all remember my fiancée, Miss Adelaide. She's here today to give you all something that's very good for your health. Adelaide, please take over.'

Adelaide smiled sweetly at the same seven children she'd met the previous week as she explained what she had in mind. 'My father's a doctor at the London Hospital, and he's taught me a lot about the health of young people like yourselves, and in particular some of the things that can make you ill or uncomfortable. Some of you, for example, may find that you're always having to scratch your head because it itches. I can make that go away, if you'd just like to take it in turns to sit in this chair.'

The children formed a polite line, and one by one Adelaide got them to sit in the chair, then lean forward over a piece of plain paper while she took a comb repeatedly through their hair. Matthew stood watching from the side, and even he could see the tiny dark objects that landed on the paper with a barely audible plop, then could be seen wriggling if one concentrated one's eyes on them. After each ritual combing, Adelaide opened a bottle by her side and rubbed a purple liquid into the scalp of every child with the aid of a cloth. Matthew had painful memories of just such a liquid being poured into a series of open scratches on his face in the early days of his relationship with Adelaide, and took a guess that it was iodine, a fact that Adelaide confirmed at the end of the class, which she had watched from the side, as if examining Matthew's teaching technique.

Just as Matthew was announcing that the children were free to leave, Clarrie Hopgood raised a tentative hand and asked, 'Will our 'eads stay this purple colour forever?'

'No,' Matthew reassured her. 'I had some of that stuff put on my face once, and it washed out in only a few weeks.'

'Me Mam only lets me wash once a week,' Clarrie replied sadly, 'so I s'pose I'll need ter look like a turkey cock till I gets ter be twelve.'

Over the course of the next few weeks, Matthew's Junior Bible Class slowly increased in attendance numbers. Each of the new attendees proved to be a working-class child with headlice, and by the end of September there were almost twenty of the junior parishioners proudly sporting purple heads, almost as if it had become a fashion statement among the youngsters.

4

Barely two weeks before his wedding date, Matthew was going over his choice of hymns for his forthcoming Evensong when the vicar, the Reverend Joseph Mulholland, entered the church by its rear door.

'What can I do for you?' Matthew asked.

Mulholland looked uncomfortable. 'It's about that fiancée of yours, Matthew,' he finally explained. 'This is rather difficult, but I'd be obliged if you'd tactfully dissuade her from any more doctoring of parish children.'

'And why might that be?' asked a perplexed Matthew.

'She painted some of their heads purple, did she not?'

'Indeed she did,' Matthew replied proudly. 'It's called iodine, and she tells me that it's a far more effective treatment for headlice than the old method using a mixture of vinegar and lard. Why, is there a problem?'

'There most certainly is,' Mulholland replied with a frown. 'She's succeeded in emphasising the social gulfs within our congregation. You may have forgotten, in your enthusiasm to allow your fiancée to play at doctors and nurses, that my great mission here has always been to create a united congregation, free of all class distinction, as Jesus originally intended. We now have a parish divided very visibly, along class lines, by the colour of their heads. I'm surprised she didn't shave them as well.'

'She really only meant the best…'

'I have no doubt that she did, but I'd be grateful if you'd dissuade her from any more well-meaning attempts to demonstrate that women can practise medicine just as well as men. I've had one formal complaint from an important lady from our congregation who seems to have formed the belief that Miss Carlyle is some sort of Suffragist, and is demanding that she be excluded from worship in our humble church. I don't recall seeing her at any of our services anyway, but that's not quite the point. I can hardly be seen to turn a blind eye to such things once she's the curate's wife, so you might wish to curb her enthusiasm.'

'Adelaide's her own woman,' Matthew protested, 'and it's a vital element of our relationship that I don't seek to dominate her in any way, or dictate what she may, or may not, do.'

'That's clearly a matter between the two of you, and I don't presume to interfere,' Mulholland insisted, 'but I can't afford to have influential women from our local community lodging formal complaints against the curate's wife.'

'It was Mrs Holroyd, wasn't it?' Matthew asked accusingly.

Mulholland shrugged. 'The identity of the lady must obviously remain confidential.'

'Adelaide put her in her place when she all but attacked poor little Tommy Tideswell and damaged his ear. She was angry because he wouldn't tell her where her son Edgar had vanished to, although if I were to be unkind I'd venture to suggest that if she were my mother I'd be wanting to escape as well.' Mulholland lowered his brow disapprovingly, and Matthew wisely moved the conversation on. 'Has Edgar come home yet?' he asked.

'No, I'm afraid not. The poor woman's obviously going frantic with worry, since it's been almost two weeks now, and apparently he liked to play by water, so she's naturally apprehensive that he might have drowned in the Thames.'

'I'll be sure to seek her out and offer her some words of comfort and support,' Matthew promised, earning a rapid shake of the head from the vicar.

'I'd rather you kept your distance from her just for the time being. And please ensure that your fiancée doesn't give the congregation any other cause for complaint.'

Matthew was in a quandary as he waited inside the church for Adelaide to arrive for their daily meeting. The wedding was only two weeks away, and Matthew and Adelaide were enjoying a carefree — almost childlike — period as they visited West End department stores, selecting furnishings, curtains, carpets and kitchen appliances and watching them being delivered and installed in their new home.

The new house was all but complete, and Adelaide was now a happy and almost frivolous young lady who gave every indication that she was eager to become a wife and mother, and he was sure that one of the contributing factors to that was that she didn't see Matthew as a threat to her independence. But now it seemed that he had to wield the heavy hand over her actions, and in effect ban her from offering nursing services to the children under his spiritual care.

'And precisely what function do you expect me to fulfil as the curate's wife?' Adelaide demanded angrily when Matthew passed on Mulholland's instructions. 'Flower arranging? Learning to play the organ? Ironing your fancy dress costumes for the services? Boiling your dog collars?'

'Look, I don't like it any more than you do,' Matthew pointed out. 'But once we can win Mrs Holroyd and her like round to your point of view, and prove just how much the parish children would benefit from proper medical attention…'

'So I have to bow my head in supplication to that dreadful woman, do I?' Adelaide demanded, red in the face, and with hands on hips in a gesture of defiance. 'Perhaps I should ask her permission to marry you in the first place — always assuming that I still want to!' With that she stormed out into the churchyard, with the departing threat of: '*If* I return tomorrow, we'll need to reconsider my role in your life!'

Matthew knew that part of her reason for agreeing to marry into the Church was the prospect of playing nurse to the parish children, and somehow he'd have to smooth things over with both the vicar and that dreadful Mrs Holroyd before he could even begin to hope that she'd return. The last thing that Adelaide Carlyle would consent to would be to adopt the second fiddle position in an organisation that she'd learned to despise, and she needed very little excuse to run back to her father and continue her more fulfilling life as his assistant. He murmured a prayer for God's merciful intervention in a mess that was not of his making, but was startled out of his mumbling when Adelaide reappeared, soaked to the skin.

'Matthew, quickly!' she shouted. 'In the churchyard, up against a gravestone — there's a young boy out there, and I don't think he's got long to live!'

Matthew raced outside, oblivious to the pounding rainstorm, following Adelaide to where she pointed down at the crumpled heap of a young boy lying with his head against a memorial plinth at the head of a grave.

Adelaide leaned down and felt the boy's neck, then looked back up at Matthew, urgent concern written across her face. 'His pulse is weak,' she told him, 'and unless we get him in out of this dreadful weather, he'll likely expire from exposure to the elements. Give me a hand, and at least we can find a useful purpose for your new house.'

His heart heavy with the implications of her use of the word 'your', Matthew took hold of the boy's legs, while Adelaide held him by the shoulders, and between them they managed to stagger to Curate's House through the mud and the pouring rain.

Once inside, Adelaide instructed that the boy be carried upstairs and laid on the mattress in what had been intended as their main bedroom. Then she pulled off her topcoat, and insisted that Matthew remove his jacket. They were both draped over the shivering boy, whose breaths were coming in short rasping bursts.

Adelaide looked up at Matthew. 'Does the vicar have a telephone installed?'

'I think so — why?'

'Because I need to contact Father urgently. If he's not still at the hospital, he'll be on his way home, but I can't deal with this until I know what the poor boy's suffering from. I only hope that your superior remembers me, and doesn't send me away as a mere meddling woman playing at being a doctor. You stay here, and if the boy regains consciousness ask him if he hurts anywhere, and how he came to be in the churchyard. If you want to do something useful, get those wet clothes off him and cover him back over with those new curtains we hung last week.'

With that she hurried down the stairs, and Matthew found himself staring down at a bedraggled youth of around twelve years of age, shivering fit to burst and murmuring inaudible words in some sort of delirium. As instructed, he stripped off the boy's clothing, noting in passing how thin and frail-looking he was, then pulled the bedroom curtains from their rods and rolled the boy up in them. As he did so, he reflected sadly that they were probably fulfilling a more valuable purpose like this than they would in the house of a bachelor curate jilted by his bride to be two weeks before she even made it to the altar.

After what seemed like an eternity there was the sound of voices from downstairs, and the heavy clomp of two people moving hastily up the stairs. Adelaide was the first to appear in the bedroom doorway, closely followed by Mulholland.

'Has there been any change?' Adelaide asked urgently.

Matthew shook his head. 'No. He occasionally tries to say something, but I can't make out what. He seems to have stopped shivering at least.'

Mulholland came to the foot of the bed and looked down. 'God be praised!' he said. 'That's Edgar Holroyd. I must summon his mother without delay.'

'Not yet,' Adelaide insisted. 'There's a very good chance that he's got a fever, and when my father gets here he may decide to administer some sort of treatment that she might find upsetting. Also, I gather from Matthew that she regards me as some sort of interfering old witch. At least wait until my father's seen him. I managed to contact him at home, and he's on his way in his coach.'

Matthew and Adelaide sat on either side of the bed, while Mulholland pulled up a chair and sat at its foot. In the uneasy silence that was broken only by Edgar's hoarse breathing, Matthew muttered a few prayers, while Mulholland sat silently watching as Adelaide periodically tested the boy's neck pulse and placed her head on his chest in the hope of hearing a heartbeat.

After almost an hour there was a heavy pounding on the outside door, and Adelaide slipped down to admit her father. He strode into the bedroom carrying his medical bag, and Matthew briefly introduced him to the vicar. Carlyle nodded in acknowledgment and reached into his bag for a stethoscope with which he listened to the boy's heart. He nodded to himself, then extracted a short glass object which he inserted under the boy's armpit.

He looked up at Adelaide. 'I think it's just a fever, but the axillary reading should confirm that.'

A few moments later he removed the tube and examined the marking on its side. 'As I suspected,' he confirmed with a further glance in Adelaide's direction. 'He has a very high temperature reading, but with the right sort of nursing he should make a full recovery. My initial suspicion is pneumonia, or perhaps something more pernicious, but the symptoms are those of a fever, and there appears to be no skin rash as yet. His heart's healthy enough, and the pulse rate gives no cause for concern. Bed rest, constant warmth, as much liquid as he can take, and an easily digested form of nutrition once he's conscious again. As you know, my preference is for beef tea in cases such as this, but whatever you can find will no doubt serve the purpose. Expect him to regain consciousness by tomorrow morning, and don't attempt anything by mouth until he does.'

'Are you intending to leave him in the care of your daughter?' Mulholland asked with what sounded like concern in his voice.

Carlyle nodded. 'I most certainly am. For one thing, I have other matters to attend to tomorrow at the London Hospital, and for another, I can't think of anyone better to assign to the straightforward task of nursing a sick boy with a fever.'

'There have been concerns expressed locally regarding your daughter's determination to do a man's job,' the vicar ventured to tell him.

'Whoever is expressing those opinions is clearly not only ignorant of my daughter's abilities, but also betraying their own short-sightedness. And so I bid you a good evening.'

It fell briefly silent, apart from the sound of Carlyle's boots descending the stairs.

'May I stay here and look after Edgar?' Adelaide asked of Mulholland.

He nodded. 'Of course. Matthew resides with us, as you'll be aware, and this house will be under your management in two weeks' time anyway. I'll get my wife to bring you over some tea and buns to tide you over, then please feel free to join us for breakfast at eight tomorrow morning. It's obviously high time that we got to know each other better.'

Once the vicar had taken his leave, Matthew followed Adelaide's instructions regarding the management of their patient, and at her request took down the curtains from the living room, to exchange for the slightly damp ones that Edgar was still wrapped in. Then he went in search of some wood and paper, with which he lit the fire in the main bedroom.

Beatrice Mulholland arrived with a pot of tea and a plate of buttered scones as promised, and once they had eagerly consumed them Matthew and Adelaide sat on either side of the bed, watching their patient for signs that he might be regaining consciousness.

After a brief while, Matthew could no longer keep quiet regarding the thoughts running through his head. 'I must own that I hadn't expected our first night in this room to take quite the form that it has,' he murmured nervously.

Adelaide smiled back across the bed at him. 'Neither had I,' she admitted, 'but it's perhaps as well for this young boy that we had it available.'

'When the vicar said that you'd be in charge of this house in two weeks' time, I didn't have the heart to tell him that you might have had a change of mind.'

'Perhaps as well that you didn't,' Adelaide replied, 'since he might change *his* mind if I don't actually kill young Edgar here with my meddling. If you formed the impression that I'd changed my mind about marrying you, then that was your mistake. I love you, Matthew West, and I can't think of a better father for my children in time to come. You won't escape me that easily. So stop moping and put some more wood on that fire.'

Matthew did as instructed with a lighter heart, then as he finished and stood back upright he felt Adelaide's arms slip around him from behind, with her head pressed against his neck. 'I thought you knew me better than that, my darling,' she whispered. 'I go off like a firework when I'm challenged wearing my woman's hat, as you've had cause to note in the past, but that doesn't mean that I don't love you. Of *course* I still want to marry you.'

They took it in turns to sleep, and it was Matthew who shook Adelaide awake where she lay on the carpet under the window when Edgar appeared to be coming to, just as the grey dawn of the new day became visible from somewhere over the distant roofs of Limehouse. She scrambled to her feet and made her way to the bed, where Edgar's eyes had half opened. He looked up at Adelaide first, then transferred his gaze to Matthew, and asked, 'Am I in the vicar's house?'

'No, my house,' Matthew told him. 'I'm the new curate, but I don't believe we've actually been introduced. I'm told that you're Edgar Holroyd — is that right?'

'Yes, that's me,' Edgar replied, then coughed and began to shiver. 'How did I get here, and who's she?' he asked as he looked back up at Adelaide.

'She's my fiancée, Adelaide,' Matthew said. 'She found you lying on a grave outside, and we brought you in here to warm you up. You were cold and wet, and the doctor says you have a fever.'

'Are you hungry?' Adelaide asked.

'Not really — more thirsty,' Edgar replied, and Matthew was sent down to the kitchen to get a glass of water.

Adelaide took one look at the colour of the water in the glass that he brought back upstairs and ordered him to open the bedroom window and tip it out. 'If that's the quality of the local water,' she tutted, 'no wonder people around here get ill so often. Do we have the gas installed yet?'

'I believe so,' Matthew replied, and was sent back down to the kitchen to boil a pot of water on the gas cooker top and bring it back for Edgar.

As he drank it eagerly, Matthew asked Edgar where he'd been for the best part of three weeks, but the boy shook his head. 'Can't tell you,' he muttered almost under his breath.

'Can't tell us because you can't remember, or because you don't want to?' Matthew persisted.

Edgar continued to shake his head. 'I daren't,' he told them, 'else the man'll kill me.'

'What man?' Adelaide asked.

Edgar looked back up at her with pleading eyes. 'You've taken all this trouble to save my life, but it'd be wasted if I told you, because he'd seek me out and have me done in, honest he would!'

Tears began to form in his eyes, and the coughing recommenced, so Adelaide placed a comforting hand on his wrist and assured him that she wouldn't ask him any more questions.

'But we'll be letting your mother know that you're safe and well, and she's bound to ask you the same,' Matthew reminded him.

Edgar shook his head. 'She's not as tough as she likes to think.'

Once it was fully light, they heard the sound of movement downstairs, and Joseph Mulholland called them down into the kitchen, where he had a full tray of breakfast laid out on the table. 'Beatrice says if you want anything else, just let me know. How's the patient?'

'He's awake and talking,' Adelaide told him, 'but I think he'd benefit from a nice sweet cup of this tea. Please thank your wife most deeply for her generosity.'

'The least we could do,' Mulholland replied. 'Has Edgar said where he's been all this time?'

'We *did* ask, but he seems reluctant to divulge any answer,' Matthew replied.

Mulholland sighed. 'Let's hope he changes his mind when his mother starts enquiring, then we might get some clue as to where the others might be.'

'The others?' Matthew echoed.

Mulholland nodded. 'There are two more children missing: young Bertie Jackson, who's a friend of Edgar's, and Clarrie Hopgood, who's in your Junior Bible Class, of course. She likes to play with the better class children like Edgar and Bertie, but they began to poke fun at her because of her purple scalp, and she seems to have reacted badly to all the ribbing, and run away.' He turned to Adelaide. 'That was your doing, I'm told, and I apologise for having reacted rather stupidly to what you were about. Since quite a lot of the parish children now have the same appearance it doesn't seem to be all that remarkable anymore, and I managed to convince quite a few of those who were complaining — including Mrs Holroyd — that since they could at least be certain that their own offspring wouldn't now be in danger of acquiring headlice, it was safe to let them mix with the poorer children.'

'Several of them have now joined my Bible Class,' Matthew announced proudly. 'But talking of Mrs Holroyd, we must perhaps let her know that Edgar's safe and well.'

'Safe, certainly,' Adelaide told them both, 'but he's still far from well, and will need careful nursing, and special foods that may be beyond the means of his parents.'

Mulholland smiled. 'That won't be a concern for the Holroyds, since they're one of our wealthier families. Tom Holroyd owns the leather business on the High Street, and he's one of our sidesmen for the Sunday morning services that I hope you'll be sharing with me before much longer. So if — Adelaide, isn't it? — says that Edgar can be safely moved, then I can give his family the good news.'

'Let's hope his rather formidable mother can reveal where he's been for these past two weeks,' Matthew said, 'since it may well be that wherever that is we may find the other missing children there.'

'My father should perhaps look him over again before he's moved,' Adelaide told them both. 'I could take the bus to the hospital after nine o'clock, and then the family coach could bring us both back here.'

'I wouldn't hear of it,' Mulholland insisted. 'The Beveridges run a coach business, and often make a vehicle available to us for parish business. I'll get Amos to call over here and provide transport for the return trip. Then once your father's seen

Edgar again, and given his approval, I'll give the glad tidings to the Holroyds.'

Adelaide was back within a couple of hours with her father, who performed various routine procedures with the patient, then gave his opinion. 'The crisis has clearly passed, and I believe that it was indeed pneumonia, since I can see no evidence of any lingering rash. The boy can be transferred to his home, provided that he's warmly wrapped for the journey. Then his mother must be advised to keep him in bed for at least three more days, and feed him beef tea or its equivalent until the appetite returns, and thereafter as much healthy sustenance as he can stomach. He will have lost quite a bit of his natural body weight during his illness, and will need to rebuild his strength before he's allowed out of bed. I'll leave you to pass on all that to the boy's mother, and I'll expect to see Adelaide back at the hospital sometime today. By the look of this place, Matthew will be kept busy re-hanging those curtains.'

Carlyle duly took his departure, and Mulholland hurried off to give the Holroyds the good news, leaving Adelaide and Matthew staring at each other across the kitchen table.

Adelaide frowned at Matthew. 'What do you know about cleaning curtains?'

'About as much as *you* know about the Pentecost,' Matthew replied.

'Well, you can't just throw curtains of that quality into a tub of soap and water,' Adelaide insisted. 'They're of the same material as those we have at home, and there's a specialist shop in Hoxton where we have ours cleaned. They use turpentine, so when you get them back and re-hang them, mind and keep the windows open for a day or two, or the fumes will make you sick. And even though I know you don't smoke, make sure that no-one comes near them with a pipe, or one of those new-fangled cigarette things that Constance is always putting in her mouth. Father once nearly succeeded in burning the house down when he stood next to our newly cleaned sitting room curtains smoking a cigar. Turpentine's highly inflammable, you see.'

'Where exactly in Hoxton is this shop?'

'You needn't worry about that,' Adelaide assured him, 'because it's time I began playing the housewife. I'll get Collins to bring the coach down here and collect them, and take them up there myself. Just make sure you're here to assist me when they need to be re-hung.'

There was a commotion at the kitchen door, and the excited exclamations of a woman whose voice they both recognised, as Mulholland flung open the door to reveal the tear-streaked countenance of Florence Holroyd. She demanded, 'Where is he?' then raced up the staircase, from which her joyful shouts and praises to God were clearly audible to those downstairs, who now included a somewhat embarrassed Thomas Holroyd, carrying a clothing bag that his wife commanded him to bring upstairs.

A few minutes later, a fully dressed Edgar Holroyd was led gingerly downstairs on his father's arm, fully dressed but with his best Sunday suit hanging off him.

'He's lost a lot of weight,' Mrs Holroyd announced accusingly.

Adelaide nodded. 'Hardly surprising in the circumstances. He's just recovering from pneumonia, so my father — the doctor — left a whole series of instructions for his immediate welfare.' Adelaide proceeded to list them, and Mrs Holroyd nodded. 'Those came from a proper doctor, you say — not just you?'

'Excuse me,' Matthew couldn't help interjecting, 'my fiancée may not be a "proper doctor", as you term it, but she's a doctor's daughter, and she knows more about medicine than you and I put together. Without her knowledge and Christian charity, you'd be collecting your son in a coffin. I believe that an apology is now in order.'

There were several sharp intakes of breath, not least from Joseph Mulholland, but as Adelaide stood politely awaiting a response, Mrs Holroyd nodded grudgingly. 'I'm sorry I misjudged you, my dear, and I hope that you enjoy perfect happiness when you marry our curate. Now I need to get this precious child home without delay. Please thank your father for me, as well.'

'I'll be sure to do that,' Adelaide assured her, then sidled up to Matthew as their visitors departed through the kitchen door. 'Thank you for that, you lovely man. It felt so good to hear you defending me like that.'

5

'How's the patient?' Carlyle asked as Adelaide walked back into the mortuary in the basement of the London Hospital, pecked her father on the cheek, then nodded casually in acknowledgment of the presence of Jennings in the corner, twirling his hat in his hands.

'He's gone home today,' she told her father, 'since he was well enough to stand if his father supported him, and made it down the stairs without mishap. Was that in order?'

'Did you pass on my instructions regarding his nursing?'

'I did indeed, and his mother sends her grateful thanks. She also seems prepared to accept that I know what I'm doing when it comes to ensuring the best health for the youngsters in Matthew's parish, which is perhaps as well, since hers is a loud and influential voice around the place.'

'When's the wedding, again?' Jennings asked.

Adelaide smiled. 'The fourteenth of this month — the Saturday after next. You're invited, should you have the time to spare, and please feel free to bring Mrs Jennings along as well.'

'Very kind of you, I'm sure,' Jennings said. 'The good lady likes weddings, and it'll be a while before our eldest gets round to it, since she's not yet fifteen.'

'How are things in the hospital?' Adelaide asked of Carlyle, who jerked his head towards a line of sealed phials on a side bench.

'Three more suspected Scarlatina deaths on the General Admission Ward. Two of them were children, but there was also a very worrying adult death, although she turned out to be the grandmother of one of the dead children. I took the usual scrapings from the worst rash sites, and they're waiting there for you to analyse, so that we can confirm cause of death for the benefit of the families.'

'I was hoping to borrow Collins and take the curtains from our new house — the ones we wrapped the Holroyd boy in — up to Wardells in Hoxton, to have them cleaned.'

'Of course,' her father agreed, 'but perhaps you'd better listen to what Inspector Jennings here has to tell us before you head off out again. He's been waiting for your arrival ever since we opened. Although I don't suppose you can shed any more light on the mystery than I was able to.'

'Try me,' Adelaide invited him as she took a seat by the workbench.

'First of all,' Jennings asked, 'have you ever known of a child fifteen feet tall?'

'Of course not!' Adelaide replied, half laughing at such a suggestion, but not sure that this would be regarded as an appropriate response.

Jennings frowned. 'Then there goes one explanation. That throws us back onto more wild speculation.'

'And why me?'

'Well, with your intended being a clergyman and all, he might be more familiar with — well, with "ghosts", and that sort of thing.'

'I'm sure he's not,' Adelaide replied on Matthew's behalf.

'I can only repeat what I already told your father, in the hope that he could assist,' Jennings began. 'In the past few weeks, there's been a series of burglaries in the lower East End. Limehouse, Wapping and Stepney, in the main. All of them older buildings that have been converted into sets of rooms for the more wealthy in the community, many of whom own the businesses on the ground floors — chandlers, ironmongers, metal turners and the like.'

'Nothing unusual so far,' Adelaide commented.

Jennings nodded his agreement. 'Until I tell you that each burglary was effected by means of entry to a room — usually a bedroom — at least twelve feet above ground. The higher buildings in those areas were all built to a pattern in the middle years of the century, and have the same design and specification, so that in the main the rooms on the upper floors that were accessed can be reckoned to be fifteen feet or so off the ground. Some a little higher, but none of them any lower than twelve feet. At that height, the occupiers felt safe in leaving their windows open to let in the breeze from the river on hot nights.'

Adelaide grimaced. 'That's not all they'd let in. The river's full of human waste, as you're well aware, and at low tide in the hot months of the year the stink is overpowering. We can even smell it some days outside here, as far north as Whitechapel. Leaving your windows open in those circumstances is likely to expose you to all manner of disgusting infections, not to mention the nausea engendered by the stench.'

'Quite,' Jennings conceded. 'But in the cases to which I'm referring, the victims also exposed themselves to felonious entry by persons unknown, who only stole small items such as jewellery, coins left by the bedsides of their sleeping victims, and — curiously — food items such as fruit and cakes. Nothing more nutritious such as meat or fish, but the sort of thing that a child might be attracted to. And that ties in with the footprints that we found on several of the window sills of the invaded houses.'

'Children's footprints, presumably?' was Adelaide's intelligent guess.

Jennings nodded. 'Bare feet, anyway. We reckon someone of between ten and thirteen years of age. Possibly the same child in each case. At least, we hope it's a child, because the alternative is unthinkable.'

'The alternative being what?' Adelaide asked, but her father intervened.

'Don't get on to that yet, Inspector, without telling Adelaide about the most remarkable feature of these burglaries — the one that has led to the public panic.'

'Yes, quite,' Jennings agreed as he continued. 'You're probably already assuming — as we did — that some agile child had been sent to scale the building, using drainpipes and suchlike in order to climb the necessary twelve or fifteen feet. Again, however, the standard design of these buildings — many of which were not originally constructed as houses, remember — has resulted in what are politely referred to as "the usual offices" being confined to the rear of the premises. In short, there are no unsightly drainpipes or other "service" devices on the front, where those residents who suffered burglaries had their bedrooms.'

'I think I now understand the reason for your seemingly bizarre question earlier regarding children fifteen feet tall,' Adelaide responded with a puzzled expression. 'Somehow or other, someone leaving the bare footprint of a person aged no older than fourteen has succeeded in gaining access to an open window fifteen feet from the ground without any climbing aid.'

'But that's not the least of his problems,' Carlyle commented.

Jennings nodded resignedly. 'There's the public panic, which is why my superiors have allocated the matter to me, after my supposed success in hosing down all that rubbish about Plague Pit demons last year, which was really all down to Doctor Carlyle and yourself.'

'And my fiancé,' Adelaide reminded him.

'I don't suppose he can come up with something to suppress the public's fears regarding the return of "Spring Heeled Jack"?' Jennings asked gloomily.

Adelaide was tempted to giggle, then restrained herself when she realised that Jennings was serious. 'Who might he be?' she asked.

It was her father who supplied the answer. 'Before your time, and indeed his earliest exploits were before even mine. He's reported as being a creature some ten feet tall, with long talons, spitting flame and capable of bounding over high walls and across rooftops in order to evade capture. He seems to have specialised in attacking young women — servant girls in the main — and tearing at their clothing in what seems to have been the preliminaries to ravishing them in laneways, on lonely heathland, or on one occasion at the front door of the house in which the terrified girl was employed.'

'Horrible!' Adelaide whispered. 'But surely this was all the product of wild imaginations, or perhaps the excuse given by the girls in question for returning home with their clothing ripped?'

'You'd have to hope so,' Jennings agreed, 'but it didn't end there, and neither was it confined to London. He was next heard of in Brighton, then he seems to have transferred his activities to Northampton, parts of East Anglia, and then as far away as Devon. The reports were all remarkably similar in general terms, although they varied in the minor details. The "man", or whatever it was, was very tall, capable of great feats of acrobatics, emitted flame, and had long talons with which he attempted to tear the clothing from girls he came across walking in lonely alleyways, or on public commons. He also took to holding up coaches along various highways.'

'But from what you're telling me,' Adelaide reasoned out loud, 'this was many years ago, and surely he'd be dead by now?'

Her father gave a hollow laugh as he took up the point. 'If this creature has such strange powers — powers that enable him to spit flame and bound over high walls and suchlike — who's to say that another of his talents isn't longevity? And in any case, he was still around when I first came to London.'

'That's right,' Jennings confirmed. 'He was active in the Peckham area in the late 1870s, and caused considerable difficulty for the soldiers in Aldershot Barracks, several of whom shot at him. Their bullets seemingly went straight through him, and he kept coming at them, forcing them to run for their very lives. He was last heard of way up north, in the Liverpool area, but London folk have long memories.'

'And bear in mind,' Carlyle added, 'that the story was embellished and leaped upon by purveyors of low fiction, playwrights, street corner sellers of trashy broadsheets and suchlike. There were plays performed about him, cheap novels featuring a similar character who ravished women on a nightly basis, and more than one lunatic who claimed to be him when apprehended for crimes such as burglary or assaults with intent to ravish.'

'So imaginative people are now claiming that this pantomime demon has returned, are they?' Adelaide asked with a sceptical giggle.

Jennings frowned. 'Don't dismiss the matter so lightly. There's genuine panic out there, and even if Spring Heeled Jack doesn't actually exist, it won't be long before people begin to claim to have seen him. He'll also be used as an excuse for other crimes — "I killed the man because he came at me out of the shadows, and I mistook his hands for talons". That sort of thing.'

'And you were hoping that I could solve your problem by leading you to a child fifteen feet tall?' Adelaide asked. 'Why should I, when you declined to investigate a relatively simple matter of one circus performer being murdered by another? Remember that one? I don't suppose it's of the remotest interest to you, but we now have a motive for murder. The man who died had fathered a child on the young girl in the family act, and the man who failed to catch him — the man who almost certainly greased his hands for that purpose — is the father of that young girl. He's also run away.'

'You bring me the answer to Spring Heeled Jack, and I'll investigate your so-called murder,' Jennings replied sourly. 'But I suppose you'll tell me that you're too busy preparing for your wedding.'

'And why not?' Adelaide countered. 'Marrying Matthew West will bring huge changes to my life, and it's hardly the place of a curate's wife to go hunting bogey-men through the lower East End. But don't think that this curate's wife won't carry on investigating the murder of Robert Manston, who left behind a fatherless child and a girl grieving in the early months of her pregnancy. That's far more down to earth and demanding of investigation than some music hall demon. Now, if you'll excuse me, I have some work to do confirming that those who pay for your services are dying of Scarlatina.'

For Adelaide, the next two weeks passed all too quickly, as she made every effort to keep up with her medical work in the mortuary, so as to not leave her father short-handed for the three weeks of her planned honeymoon. There were also the last-minute details that required her attention, such as the guest lists, the seating plans for the reception in a giant marquee in the grounds of St Dunstan's, and of course the travel plans for the honeymoon. She was reluctant to inflict any of this on Matthew, since he had his hands more than full getting into full stride as the curate in a busy East End parish, and in any case, she was a better organiser than he was, and much of the detail that required to be addressed came as the result of her Irish connections.

Her late mother Kathleen had been one of three children born to a relatively wealthy grain merchant in Newtownards, south-east of Belfast. Her parents were dead, so Adelaide had no grandparents on her mother's side, but she had an uncle and aunt who had both prospered and multiplied. First of all her mother's older brother, Jack O'Brien, who was a wealthy farmer in a place called Mount Stewart, on the shores of Strangford Lough. Adelaide had fond memories of several long summers spent playing with her two female cousins, Mary and Bridey, in the halcyon days before her mother caught the fever and passed quickly out of her life.

There was also Adelaide's Aunt Maggie and her husband and family in Bangor, on the coast a few miles north-east of Belfast, where Uncle Padraig ran a fleet of fishing vessels out into the Irish Sea. They had two strapping boys who Adelaide remembered largely for their habit of pulling at her long red hair — a legacy from her mother — and chasing her into the sea while threatening her with live crabs and lobsters. They would be men now, but would no doubt still be offended if they were not invited to the wedding.

Matthew rapidly came to realise that on his day of days he would be seriously outnumbered by the Irish contingent, and in any case he had few relatives outside his own immediate family. Brother Charles was the obvious best man for the wedding, and given his love of showing off he was delighted to take on the task. Matthew's sister Caroline, coming on nineteen years of age, would make a perfect bridesmaid along with Adelaide's cousins Mary and Bridey, and this left Adelaide's lifelong friend Constance Wilberforce as Matron of Honour. The service was to be conducted by the vicar of St Dunstan's, Joseph Mulholland, so that all the formalities had fallen neatly into place.

There had been considerable discussion over where to spend the honeymoon until the O'Briens had replied accepting their wedding invitations, and insisting that Adelaide and Matthew spend their first three weeks of married life as their guests on the farm at Mount Stewart. There were several cottages on the slopes overlooking Strangford Lough, one of which was for the use of a farm manager, and was therefore more comfortably equipped than the average farm labourer's cottage. The O'Briens were currently 'between managers', the cottage was vacant, and the O'Briens refused to take no for an answer, so that was the honeymoon location taken care of.

Matthew had been left in charge of the travel arrangements, and had spent several weeks scratching his head in frustration until his brother Charles had come to the rescue and travelled across the city to Euston Station, returning with handfuls of brochures regarding the delights to be enjoyed while travelling across country by rail to the Port of Liverpool, there to take a night ferry across the Irish Sea to Belfast, where they could be met by the O'Brien coach and taken south to their idyllic honeymoon cottage. Matthew purchased the necessary tickets, and then and only then gave Adelaide the good news regarding the travelling arrangements he'd made.

In her own highly practical way, but conscious of the effort that Matthew had made to take at least some of the arrangements out of her hands, Adelaide tactfully pointed out that since they were to be married at 11 a.m. on the 14th, and that the subsequent reception would no doubt last until the middle of the afternoon, they would not be able to catch the departing train from Euston on that day. A red-faced Matthew had succeeded in getting the tickets exchanged for equivalents on the Monday — since the service was unavailable on the Sunday — and this just left the question of where they were to spend their first two nights as Mr and Mrs West.

Urgent enquiries, and another trip west by brother Charles, revealed the existence of a first-class hotel at Euston Station, at which they could stay on the Sunday night prior to enjoying a late leisurely breakfast ahead of the train journey to Liverpool, and the somewhat challenging prospect of a double berth across a hopefully tame Irish Sea. This left the Saturday night, and the happy couple were content to spend their wedding night in the now completed Curate's House, to which they retired after an emotionally draining day in which they had made their vows, been toasted by their respected families, and waved goodbye to their final guests just as the sun was beginning to dip below the distant dome of St Paul's, to their west.

They came downstairs on the Sunday morning to the delightful smells of breakfast being cooked in their kitchen by the kindly Beatrice Mulholland, who refrained from asking them any question that might even vaguely be taken as a reference to their first night together when she saw the slightly dreamy looks on their faces, and remembered her own wedding night some twenty odd years in the past.

The train journeys and sea crossings in each direction, and the almost three weeks spent gazing down at the pristine waters of Strangford Lough, testing the salt waters at Bangor, and enjoying Ulster hospitality at its most fulsome, would rank as some of the happiest times they had ever known, but there came a day when the coach they had hired at Euston dropped them off at the gates to St Dunstan's churchyard, and they began to heave their travelling bags up the long drive.

Even that seemed to have been taken care of, as a team of four robust lads from the parish appeared out of the church hall, accompanied by the vicar and his wife with broad smiles of welcome at their return. The boys lifted their bags and ran them up to their house on the far side of the churchyard, leaving Joseph and Beatrice Mulholland to chat happily to them all about their honeymoon, exchanging their accounts of three weeks in Ulster for trivia regarding events in the parish.

When they reached the house, Adelaide was almost reduced to tears upon learning that Beatrice Mulholland had filled the kitchen cupboards with all the supplies they would need until they could make their way to the local shops, and for which she blankly refused payment. Adelaide was excitedly opening cupboards, expressing her delight at what she found in there, and gratefully accepting the Mulhollands' invitation to join them for supper in the vicarage, when Joseph Mulholland beckoned with a faint hand gesture for Matthew to accompany him outside.

As they stood in the shadow of the front porch, the vicar's face lost its previous welcoming smile. 'You're going to need the happy memories of your honeymoon when you resume parish duties, which will presumably be tomorrow,' he told Matthew.

'Something bad's happened, hasn't it?' Matthew asked anxiously.

Mulholland nodded. 'There are now a total of twelve children missing from the parish, and Mrs Vane is insistent that she's been visited by the ghost of hers.'

'Did they all disappear at the same time, or over a period?' Matthew asked over the supper table.

Mulholland frowned. 'That's one of the difficulties. The parents have been very reluctant to report the children missing — possibly because they felt that they were in some way being criticised as parents — and given that there have been no meetings of your Junior Bible Class while you've been away, it wasn't until we had the delayed Harvest Festival service, and Mrs Caxton began assembling the children for the traditional costume parade, that we learned of the disappearances.'

'So for all we know they may each have gone for different reasons?' Adelaide observed.

Mulholland shook his head. 'That would be stretching coincidence too far, I feel. In the many years now that I've been the vicar here, I can only think of one or two cases of children going missing, and they were the usual rebellious "running away from home" responses that we occasionally see in our young people. And those children always came back after a day or two, when they realised how well off they were to have a roof over their heads, and regular cooked meals. These more recent disappearances, on the other hand, seem to form a pattern. In every case the child seems to have planned their "escape", if we might call it that. Removing food from the larder, taking their best clothes, warm coats, Sunday boots and so on. It's almost as if someone's been enticing them away.'

'What enquiries have you made so far?' Matthew asked.

Mulholland spread his arms in a gesture of resignation as he responded. 'We obviously called together every remaining child, and told them that if they knew anything, then it was their Christian duty to tell me, and I reassured them that they wouldn't be in any trouble. But the response was nothing but silence.'

'Have any of them since returned?' was Matthew's next question.

Mulholland shook his head. 'Only the Holroyd boy that you looked after so magnificently when he returned half dead that night. He's proved to be particularly tight-lipped, I'm afraid.'

'When we questioned him, he mentioned something about a man who'd kill him if he revealed anything,' Adelaide reminded them. 'That rather fits the abduction or enticement theory, doesn't it?'

Beatrice Mulholland shivered. 'It doesn't bear thinking about,' she said. 'You hear of such things these days, obviously — evil people who entice young children away for … well, you know what I mean.' She pulled a handkerchief from the sleeve of her blouse and began sobbing, causing her husband to place a consoling arm around her shoulders and mumble a few reassuring words. Then he looked up at Matthew.

'We were hoping that you might be able to get some more information from your Bible Class children.'

'I'll certainly try,' Matthew assured him, 'but I'm not sure that I'll have any more success than you've had.'

'You might be surprised,' Mulholland said. 'During your absence I received more than one good report about your rapport with the parish children. And not just from the children themselves.'

'Tell us more about the child who's allegedly come back from the dead,' Adelaide requested.

It was Beatrice Mulholland who supplied the answer. 'It was Mrs Vane — William's mother,' she explained. 'She's on my roster for the flower displays on the church altar, and I think she felt that she could more easily approach me than my husband. She began by asking if I believed in ghosts, and when I pooh-poohed the very idea, she came right out with it. "Well, you must be wrong," she almost shouted, "because I saw my dead William last night!" Then she burst into floods of tears and ran out of the church. That was two days ago, and I've been meaning to visit her and ask for more details, but I haven't had the time, and to be perfectly honest with you I've shrunk from doing it in case I upset her even more.'

'William Vane's one of the missing children, I take it?' Adelaide asked.

Mulholland nodded. 'He was one of the first to go missing, at about the same time as Edgar Holroyd, so he's been gone for quite a few weeks now.'

'Would you like me to speak with her?' Matthew asked.

Mulholland nodded. 'We'd both be mightily obliged to you if you would.'

'And presumably there'd be no objection to my accompanying Matthew?' Adelaide chimed in. When their hosts seemed a little uncertain as to how to respond, she added, 'As the curate's wife, surely I'll be expected to play a role in parish affairs? We haven't yet got around to discussing what that role might be, but this would seem to be a good start. I may not be a mother, but I've had some experience of children through my medical work, and of course I'm a woman, and I think I might have a better idea of what she's going through, and be better able to discover any explanation for her vision of her missing child than my husband, who can be a bit on the obtuse side sometimes.'

'No I'm not!' Matthew protested, and turned to their hosts for support. Both of them dropped their gaze to the table, and Adelaide gave a triumphant chuckle as she kissed his cheek. 'Even your greatest supporters have to admit that sometimes you have all the reasoning ability of a blancmange. One of the greatest services I can perform for this parish will be to sharpen up your analytical powers a little. We'll go and talk to Mrs Vane tomorrow.'

6

'Do I really have the brain of a blancmange?' Matthew asked as Adelaide placed the second boiled egg on his breakfast plate the following morning.

She smiled. 'In some ways, yes. But the brain is a complex organ. You have admirable strength and courage when it comes to defending something that you believe in, like your faith in God, but, as you've proved on more than one occasion, you can no more think sideways than you can ballet dance. But, this is both the first full day of our married residence in this lovely house, and also the final day that I cook breakfast. You can leave dinner and supper to me for the time being, but I'm taking a stand now, before the rot sets in. There's no biological reason why men can't cook, and some of the finest hotels in London have male chefs. It's only social convention that's led to women doing all the cooking, and this new wife has other calls on her time and talents. I don't intend to be the smiling little domestic fairy behind the big important man — the "good lady", as Inspector Jennings condescendingly calls his wife — so you'll need to share at least some of the household duties.'

'But I have parish duties to perform.'

'And I have medical responsibilities down at the hospital, in case you've forgotten. The agreement was that I'd live here with you as "Mrs West", while continuing as "Miss Carlyle" down the road in Whitechapel, remember?'

'So you won't be coming with me to speak to Mrs Vane?'

'Yes, I will, which is why the sooner you eat that second egg the better, since I'd like to take the bus down Mile End Road before dinner time. But take the time to savour it, because tomorrow's egg will have been boiled by you.'

The door opened slightly, and a pair of suspicious eyes looked out at them. They were at the side door on the ground floor of the draper's shop in Belgrave Street that was owned by Herbert Vane and his wife Lillian, and according to the instructions they had received inside the shop itself the owners were to be found living above their shop.

'Mrs Vane?' Matthew asked as softly and politely as he could. 'We haven't met formally, but you may have seen me around the parish from time to time. I'm Matthew West, the new curate, and this lady is my wife Adelaide.'

'Did the vicar's wife send you?' the mouth below the eyes enquired.

Matthew nodded. 'That's right — she said you had something to tell us about William.'

'He's dead, you know.'

'Well, we know that he's missing,' Adelaide confirmed, 'and we were hoping that you could tell us about seeing him recently.'

'I saw his ghost, certainly, but Beatrice Mulholland must have reckoned that I'd gone off my head on account of the grief, because she gave me a funny look. Why has she sent you to find out more?'

'We're here on our own account, to hear what you can tell us,' Adelaide explained. 'Mrs Mulholland didn't send us on her account; she thought that what you saw might be important in finding the other missing children.'

'You'd better come inside, then,' Lillian invited them as she opened the door wider and indicated for them to climb the stairs that led onto a landing from which she directed them into the kitchen and lit the gas under the water. Then she poured three level spoonfuls of tealeaves into a teapot at the side and placed three cups, a sugar basin and a milk jug on the table at which Matthew and Adelaide had been invited to take a seat, before producing a plate of biscuits from an overhead cupboard. 'Gingers — they were Billy's favourites, so it's only right that we eat them while we're respecting his memory,' she choked. A tear rolled down her face as she struggled to maintain control of her emotions.

Adelaide reached out to place a hand on Lillian's slightly shaking wrist. 'I don't yet have children of my own, Mrs Vane, so I won't pretend to be fully aware of the depth of your despair, but please believe me when I say that we're only here to help.'

'And to assure you of God's love always,' Matthew added piously.

Lillian smiled palely at him as she took a seat at the table. 'It must have been God's mercy that allowed me a glimpse of him as he popped back down from Heaven. Four nights ago now, it was. I woke up, and something made me look out of the window.'

'This was your bedroom window?' Adelaide asked gently.

Lillian nodded. 'That's right. The bedroom's at the front, above the shop. Bert was still asleep, but something woke me up, and I turned over and opened my eyes, and there he was.'

'Standing by your bed?' Adelaide prompted her.

'Out of the window, like I said.'

'You live above the shop,' Matthew reminded her, 'so your bedroom window must be all of fifteen feet from the ground, surely?'

'Yes,' Lillian nodded, 'which is why I know that Billy must be dead. His face was looking at me from outside the window, and he couldn't have climbed up there, obviously. It *must* have been his ghost, mustn't it?'

While Matthew appeared to be nonplussed by this answer, Adelaide had more questions. 'How long was he there for? And did you see anything of him other than his face?'

'It only lasted for a few seconds,' Lillian replied, 'and I only took in his face, since it was quite a shock, as you can imagine. I sat up in bed and called out his name, and he just sort of disappeared from sight. His face went quickly downwards, and I called out to Bert — that's my husband — and went towards the window. Then I sort of caught my feet in the bedclothes and fell onto the lino. By the time I got to the window there was no sign of Billy anywhere, and Bert told me to come back to bed because it was only a dream. Only I wasn't asleep, and I know what I saw. People *can* come back from the dead, can't they, Reverend?'

Matthew coughed awkwardly, and appeared to be at a loss for an honest answer, requiring Adelaide to take back control of the conversation.

'And you only saw him just this one time?' she asked.

'That's right — just the once. Perhaps Mrs Mulholland's right, and I'm going daft with worry. It's been a few weeks now.'

'I don't think so for one moment,' Adelaide consoled her. 'There's probably a very good reason why you caught sight of him for that brief moment, and we can only hope that it happens for you again, since it must bring you great comfort.'

'You've no idea,' Lillian agreed as she reached out and gripped Adelaide's hand. 'It probably won't be long until you have children of your own, then you'll realise only too well what we're going through. It's not just me, either — Bert's suffering just the same, but being a man he can't show it, and of course we have to keep smiling faces for the customers. Would you like more tea?'

'No, we have to be going now,' Adelaide told her as she rose from the table in a silent gesture to Matthew that they were leaving. 'Thank you so much for the tea and biscuits, and for sharing your experience with us. I can assure you that we don't think that you're losing your mind, and here's hoping that Billy visits you again.'

'You didn't seriously believe all that rubbish about Billy coming back from the dead, did you?' Matthew demanded as they walked back up towards Stepney Green, where Adelaide could continue onto Mile End Road to take the short bus journey into Whitechapel, and the hospital.

'Of course not,' Adelaide insisted, 'but as a man of God you appeared to have no answer, so I just said something reassuring in order to keep her talking. But I *can* tell you that Billy's almost certainly still alive.'

'And how would you know that?' Matthew asked as St Dunstan's came into view on their right, and he slowed the pace.

'Something that Inspector Jennings said a few weeks ago, before the wedding. He's investigating a series of burglaries of houses here in the East End, in which someone's gaining access by way of windows left open on upper floors. The only physical evidence they've managed to acquire is the footprint of a child. What age would Billy be?'

'No idea, but if he was a friend of Edgar Holroyd's when he first disappeared, he'd be about the same age as him, which I think is around twelve or thirteen.'

'That's exactly the age that Jennings reckons this child was that left a wet footprint on a window ledge somewhere down in Wapping or Limehouse.'

'So you think that this burglar might be Billy Vane?' Matthew asked. 'If so, how come his mother only saw his face, and not the rest of him? And how did he get up there in the first place?'

Adelaide stopped for a moment and looked admiringly at him. 'I do believe that at long last you're learning to think logically. You can thank me for that.'

'You didn't answer my question,' Matthew reminded her.

'That's because I don't *have* an answer. But I can add something to Jennings's investigation, can't I? We can be more certain that these burglaries were indeed the work of a child.'

'So you seriously intend to inform Jennings that Billy Vane was about to burgle his own parents' house?'

'Why not? He'd know where the valuables were to be found, anyway.'

'Why could Mrs Vane only see his face, then?' Matthew challenged her.

Adelaide frowned. 'I obviously don't know, do I? But it's better than suggesting that she was seeing his ghost. Anyway, I'll see you at supper time. Don't use up all the bread for your dinner.'

They parted at the entrance to the churchyard, and Adelaide spent her few minutes waiting for the bus service down into Whitechapel thinking over what they had learned from Mrs Vane, and tying it together with what the vicar had advised them regarding the other missing children from the parish congregation. Then she remembered Edgar Holroyd's stubborn refusal to say where he'd been, and what he'd been up to, before something had driven him back home. He'd made some vague reference to a man of whom he was terrified to speak — a man who'd kill him if he said too much.

From time to time, one heard of bands of 'ragged children' being organised into street gangs by shadowy manipulators who took what they could pickpocket, or otherwise steal from unsuspecting dupes, in return for giving them somewhere to sleep, and an occasional meal. Was this how Edgar Holroyd had finished up, and was Billy Vane still a member of such a group? If she told Inspector Jennings what she knew, would he be interested enough to pursue the matter, and perhaps rescue the parish waifs? It was to be doubted, given his reluctance to even involve himself in the obvious murder of one circus performer by another, so why waste her time? She'd have enough to do anyway, once she alighted from the bus at the hospital and descended to the basement mortuary, to be reunited with the father she hadn't seen since she kissed him farewell on her wedding day, thanking him for every day of the privileged life she'd led.

He turned as she breezed through the mortuary door, and called out, 'I hope you missed me.' He gave her a broad smile and hugged her to him. 'Life seemed very empty and pointless without you around, questioning everything I do, and there's a mountain of analysis waiting for you, most of it Scarlatina related. So how's married life treating you?'

'It's difficult to imagine how I survived without it for twenty-three years. Matthew's wonderful, and I'm gradually moulding him into the perfect husband.'

Carlyle chuckled. 'Your mother always claimed to have civilised me, but I fear that I've slipped into lazy ways since she's been gone.'

'Probably because you had a wild daughter to worry about, who's now become the sort of happily married woman that I always despised. High time that I resumed the work for which I've been trained by the best surgeon in London.'

The morning passed in a happy bubble of familiarity, and after Adelaide had confirmed that the first five phials waiting for her had indeed contained Scarlatina scrapings from the unfortunates who'd died on one of the wards on the floors above, James Carlyle offered to go out and bring back something tasty for their dinner. They were just commenting on the constant quality of the mutton pies from the Italian bakers round the corner in Turner Street when there came a heavy knock on the door, and the face of a very peeved Inspector Jennings appeared round it. He glanced first at the mutton pies in their hands, muttered, 'All right for some,' then nodded at the empty mortuary slab. 'Room for a little one?'

'What have you got for me?' Carlyle asked.

Jennings indicated the corridor behind him with a backward jerk of the head. 'A young girl, fished out of Regent's Canal at the Limehouse Basin. The Yard were called in because we've had reports of young people going wild down there of late, and some of the property owners have been complaining that it's not good for business. I need to know if she's been murdered or not, and I need this like a spare head right now. So, if you wouldn't mind?'

'Bring her in and lay her out on the slab,' Carlyle invited him.

Jennings stepped back out into the corridor for long enough to bark some curt instructions to two uniformed bobbies who between them carried the limp, dripping, and fully clothed form of a young teenaged girl into the mortuary and laid her out on the slab.

Carlyle took a cursory glance at the body, then told Jennings, 'I'll need an hour or so to see if she drowned, and if so what led to her being in the water in the first place. It's dinner time, so if you and your men would like to take advantage of the canteen on the ground floor…'

'No thank you very much,' Jennings replied as he pulled a face. 'I've tried that place before, and if you aren't ill when you come into the London Hospital in the first place, you soon will be if you eat in there. Is Nardini's still in business?'

'Where do you think these mutton pies came from?' Carlyle asked.

Jennings turned to the two constables. 'I just saved you fellows from a severe dose of the Southside Squirts. Follow me, lads, and I'll show you a *real* Cornish pastie.'

They disappeared back down the corridor, and Adelaide walked casually across from her workbench to look down at their recent delivery. Then her brows knitted in concern, and she looked back up at her father. 'I think I know this girl! Or at least, I think I met her once. I never forget a head of hair that I've scraped nits out of, and you can still see the remains of the iodine in her scalp. Is Collins still here in the staff restroom? Only I need to get Matthew down here without delay!'

Two hours later they were grouped gloomily round the sad, sodden remains of the young girl, river weed still tangled in her hair, and her cheap dress and threadbare petticoat looking like discarded rags.

'That's Clarrie Hopgood,' Matthew confirmed gloomily, 'and I suppose I'll have to break the news to her parents.'

'At least it may persuade some of the other young people in your Junior Bible Class to tell us what's been going on,' Adelaide pointed out. 'When they learn that she was probably murdered, that should loosen their tongues. Didn't Edgar Holroyd speak about a man who'd kill him if he breathed a word about where he'd been? Perhaps this poor girl tried to escape, and was done in for her efforts.'

'We don't know that she was murdered,' Carlyle reminded her. 'The symptoms are consistent with an accident.'

'She fell into the canal, and couldn't swim to the side, you mean?' Jennings asked.

Carlyle shook his head. 'I've obviously dressed the poor unfortunate girl back into the clothes she was wearing, in the belief that she would need to be identified by a grieving parent or other family member. However, I imagine that Matthew's identification will suffice for police purposes. But the clothing conceals the fact that I was obliged to open her up, and I can advise you professionally that she didn't drown.'

'How can you be sure?' Jennings asked.

It was Adelaide who displayed her understanding of post-mortem symptoms as she suggested, 'No water in the lungs?'

'Precisely,' her father confirmed. 'But her poor little body was subjected to all manner of trauma, and it may be that the combined effect of the broken bones I discovered brought on some sort of cardiac seizure?'

'She was battered to death, you mean?' Adelaide asked shakily, her hand to her mouth.

Carlyle shrugged. 'That's one theory. There's a particularly bad fracture to the side of the cranium that could have been fatal, and since she clearly wasn't breathing when she hit the water, then this might account for her death. But there are some other rather puzzling fractures.'

'Such as?' Adelaide asked, pale in the face.

Carlyle gently lifted the hem of both the dress and petticoat. 'See here. Adelaide, perhaps you'd care to describe what you see, and confirm my suspicion that this was no straightforward death.'

In a wavering voice that occasionally broke entirely, Adelaide did as requested, and Matthew and Jennings listened in mounting horror.

'Right fibula snapped anteriorly and driven hard against the patella. Left fibula driven directly through the patella, forcing it into the femur. Oh, dear God — the poor child must have been in agony!'

She could contain the tears no longer, and sobbed bitterly against Matthew's shoulder, while Jennings raised his eyebrows enquiringly at Carlyle. 'That was gibberish to me — what did it mean?'

'This is only a guess on my part, you understand?' Carlyle told him. 'But what you see there is consistent with the girl having jumped from a high place — perhaps the roof of the place in which she was being imprisoned — and breaking both legs horribly when she landed. They would not have been able to support her body weight — pitifully light though it was — and she would have crumpled to the ground. That would explain the fracture to the cranium, and as I already explained this could have killed her. That, in addition to cardiac shock brought about by the agonising pain in the lower limbs.'

'Stop it, father — it's too horrible!' Adelaide said. 'Just a slip of a girl. Her poor mother — it's too dreadful to contemplate!'

Matthew looked quizzically at Carlyle, who shrugged. Neither of them had ever seen Adelaide display such open emotion, and she had spent long enough at the dissection table assisting her father for this sort of thing not to disturb her normally. They both silently concluded that the cause of this outburst was the fact that the deceased had only been a young girl, and what's more a young girl that Adelaide had met, albeit only briefly.

'I think we all need a strong sweet cup of tea,' Carlyle announced, 'and that includes you, Adelaide. I know that you normally don't take sugar, but you look as if you could do with it on this occasion.'

She'd calmed down by the time that the tea had been served, and they were all sipping gloomily at their mugs as Jennings tried to make sense of it all.

'Well, doctor,' he finally asked, 'what do you think? Was she beaten to death, or did she fall from a great height while trying to escape from somewhere, or what?'

'The latter, if I was being forced to settle for one conclusion or the other. The broken legs could only have come from direct impact with the ground in an almost vertical plane, which is consistent with a jump. Then I asked myself why even a young, perhaps foolish, and certainly inexperienced girl would do such a thing. The most likely explanation is that she was trying to escape from something worse, which I'll leave to your imagination and experience.'

'There were no other obvious signs of injury?' Jennings asked.

Carlyle shook his head. 'Not externally, no. But there was nothing but a watery froth in her stomach, which I don't think was leftover soup. Her tongue was somewhat shrivelled, and deep red in hue. Her eyes gave some indication of a lack of red blood in her system, and her gums were spongy to the touch. I've seen those symptoms in children brought into the workhouse after being found in the gutter, and it's strongly suggestive of malnutrition. Also, given her apparent age I'd expect to see more body fat than you can see at present. All in all, this girl appears to have been starved for some period prior to her death.'

Adelaide turned to confront Jennings. 'What do you intend to do about this? An innocent young girl jumped to her death rather than be subjected to violation by some monster who's been abducting children from the Stepney area and subjecting them to Christ knows what! And don't look at me in that pathetic manner, Matthew — what did your precious God do to save this poor girl? She was on the verge of becoming a young woman, and in due course a mother. No doubt she's left a mother of her own to cry pitiful tears for her loss. You men are very good at pontificating, but where were any of you while all this was going on, and for all we know is *still* going on? What do you intend to *do* about it?'

'I'll obviously instigate enquiries...' Jennings began, only to be drowned out by Adelaide's next tirade.

'Enquiries into what? The price of meat pies? The best pub to be found in the East End?'

'Well, what do you suggest, exactly?' Jennings fought back, his rising anger visible at shirt collar level.

'Find where these poor children are being hidden away and abused! Send out every man you've got, and run them ragged until they find the reptile responsible for this. Just ... just ... *do* something!'

'Come on, Adelaide,' Matthew murmured in acute embarrassment as he took Adelaide by the arm and pulled her gently towards the door, while her father stood there open-mouthed. Her angry voice could still be heard by the two men left inside the mortuary as she was escorted down the corridor towards the stairs that led up to the ground floor.

'I can only apologise for my daughter's uncharacteristic outburst,' Carlyle mumbled in the silence that followed.

'I've heard worse, believe me. But not from a lady of breeding.'

'I've never known her get so — so "emotionally disturbed", I suppose you could call it,' Carlyle admitted.

'Your daughter had a point, though,' Jennings admitted, 'and I really will have to at least be seen to be doing something. But I'm not so recently familiar with the area around the Regent's Canal, thank God, so I'll have to rely on local knowledge, and begin preliminary enquiries, in order to see if there have been any other reports of children being seen in places where they haven't been seen in the past. A bit "needle in haystack", obviously, but at least I'll be seen to be doing something.'

'I don't think it helped that you blankly refused to make any enquiry into that suspected circus murder,' Carlyle suggested. 'There was clear evidence to suggest that the man's fall from the trapeze was anything but accidental.'

'You're right, of course, and I should have listened to you,' Jennings admitted. 'But they'll likely be miles away by now.'

'Isn't there some way of finding out where they might be?' Carlyle argued. 'Adelaide was quite concerned that the daughter of the man who went missing at the time of the incident was expecting a child, and that she might be lacking medical attention given their casual lifestyle, always on the road.'

'No idea,' Jennings admitted, 'and at the risk of sounding like a phonograph with a stuck cylinder, I'll obviously make enquiries. And now I'd better go about my business, before I receive any further unkind comments. Thank you for the tea, and good luck with your daughter.'

7

'I really think you owe Jennings an apology,' Matthew insisted gently as the coach rumbled back up the long slope towards St Dunstan's, and he plucked up the courage to say something.

'Since when was an apology needed for speaking one's mind?' Adelaide challenged him.

Matthew was ready for that. 'When one's mind is disordered through an excess of emotion over reality,' he replied.

Adelaide snorted her disagreement. 'The "reality", as you call it, is that children are being held captive somewhere by some unspeakable monster doing unspeakable things to them.'

'You don't know that,' he reasoned.

She turned to face him, red in the face. 'And *you* don't know that they're *not*, do you? As long as it's a possibility, we have to do something, because that oaf of a so-called police inspector clearly doesn't intend to. Anyway, here we are.'

Matthew climbed down from the coach, then reached in to help Adelaide out of it.

'I'm going back to the mortuary,' she insisted.

'Oh no you're not,' Matthew told her as he pulled her gently down onto the church path. 'The mood you're in, you're likely to get yourself arrested. And I still haven't mastered the art of boiling an egg. The one I had this morning had all the consistency of jellied eels, so I think I need to practise my timing.'

'I'll come home with you, as you suggest,' Adelaide agreed, 'but I really feel that I ought to lie down for a while. My head's aching after that rush of blood to it.'

Two hours later, Matthew was working on his sermon for his Sunday Evensong service when Adelaide tiptoed into his study while his attention was devoted to his notes, then wrapped her arms around him from behind and kissed the back of his head. 'I'm sorry, darling,' she murmured. 'I don't know what got into me.'

Matthew straightened his back, stood up, turned round and held her to him. 'It's not me you should be apologising to,' he reminded her, 'but it'll do for a start. You had me quite concerned for a while there, since I've never known you go off like that.'

'It was just the thought of what that poor girl's mother has facing her when you give her the awful tidings, which you'll have to do by tomorrow at the latest. I found myself wondering how I'd feel in her place, and then I thought of that poor sweet little girl, and what — well, what…'

The tears began again, and Matthew held her tightly, and reassured her that he'd break the news to Mrs Hopgood as gently as he was able. Then a thought occurred to him. 'It's just possible that when the other children hear what happened to Clarrie, they might be prepared to tell us what they know. My next Junior Bible Class is tomorrow afternoon — would you like to come with me and see if you can persuade them to part with whatever information they can give us? That way, you'll at least feel that you're doing something.'

The following afternoon, the fire seemed to have returned to Adelaide's eyes as she surveyed the twenty or so youngsters who were attending the first Junior Bible Class since the curate and his new bride had returned from their honeymoon. She cleared her throat, then let her eyes rest on each of them for a second or two as she swept them all with her gaze.

'Your parents have no doubt already told you, but you should know that young Clarrie Hopgood was found dead a few days ago. Her body was fished out of the canal down in Limehouse, but she didn't drown. It looks as if someone threw her body in there after she broke both her legs trying to escape from a tall building, or maybe over a wall, somewhere.

'As you know, she's not the only youngster from this parish who's gone missing, and the curate and I want to do what we can to prevent any more of them dying. We believe that they may have been promised something special by whoever talked them into leaving home. There are many wicked people in London, but they don't always seem to be bad when you first meet them. They may promise you sweeties, or pies, or something like that. Or they may pretend to have a horse you can ride, or a boat that you can sail on the Thames. But once they have you held captive, and you can't escape from them, they start doing very nasty things to you. So please, if you know anything about where your missing friends have gone, you *must* tell either me or my husband. You won't be in any sort of trouble, I can promise you that, but you might be saving your friends from something very awful. Thank you for listening to me, and now the curate wants to remind you of someone else who came to the rescue of someone who'd been misused, so please listen carefully.'

Matthew had craftily chosen, as his Bible theme for the day, the tale of the 'Good Samaritan', and he adapted the message that the story contained into a further appeal for information regarding the possible whereabouts of their missing friends. But despite his emphasis on the point that the Man from Samaria had earned blessings from God for coming to the aid of someone he'd never even met, the children in his class remained resolutely silent regarding the whereabouts of those whom they'd grown up alongside. Matthew concluded the class, thanking them for their attendance, and as they all filed out, Adelaide turned to Matthew with a long face.

'Whoever's taken these children must have a very firm hold on the others. It was presumably only after Edgar Holroyd came back with his fear of "the man", and the threats that he'd made, that the rest of the children became reluctant to speak.'

'Yes,' Matthew agreed, 'but what puzzles me is why even those who've never been in the man's grip seem to be afraid of him. What possible hold can he have over those who remain safe at home? Or is it more the case that they don't want their friends to be chastised by their parents for running away in the first place?'

'I doubt the latter,' Adelaide argued. 'If I were one of those parents, I'd be only too glad to see them back.'

They'd been walking down the path through the churchyard that led to the curate's house during this conversation, heads down against a stiff early autumn breeze, so they didn't notice the young girl half hidden behind a tall gravestone. As they were about to draw level with it she stepped gingerly out onto the grass, and hovered there with an uncertain look on her face.

Matthew smiled kindly at her. 'You'd better get home, Daisy, before it gets dark. Don't you want any supper?'

'It's about Clarrie,' she whispered. 'Is she really dead?'

'I'm afraid so,' Adelaide confirmed. 'I was working in the hospital with my father and I saw her body. The curate here recognised her.'

Tears formed in Daisy's eyes as she hung her head and muttered, 'She didn't mean any harm, and she wasn't being naughty.'

'Then why did she run away from home?' Matthew asked.

The answer came in a whisper. 'She ran off to join the circus.'

'The circus?' Adelaide echoed.

Daisy nodded. 'I was supposed to be going with her, but Mother caught me packing my bag and locked me in my room. Clarrie must have gone on her own.'

'Who told you about a circus?' was Adelaide's next question, but Daisy seemed reluctant to answer.

'Did a man come to Stepney looking for children to join the circus?' Matthew prompted her.

Daisy shook her head. 'I don't want to get anyone into trouble, but it perhaps doesn't matter now, because they say that Billy Vane's dead.'

'So it was Billy Vane, was it?' Adelaide persisted.

Daisy nodded. 'He went off with Edgar Holroyd weeks ago, then he came back and told us about this man who's looking for children to learn how to do things in the circus. Clarrie and a few others went off with him, and we haven't seen any of them since.'

'Do you happen to know which circus?' Adelaide asked.

Daisy shook her head. 'It was meant to be a new one that was just starting up. One that was just for children, and they were supposed to be going round the country, earning lots of money. But from what you told us in Bible Class he was a bad man, wasn't he?'

'We don't know that for certain, do we?' Adelaide said reassuringly.

Daisy shook her head. 'We just have to pray for them, I suppose. Anyway, I need to get home now.'

'Thank you *very* much for being so brave in telling us this,' Matthew beamed at her. 'God will reward your kindness and courage.'

'I hope he sends awful torments to the man who killed Clarrie,' she said as she scampered off down the path, leaving Matthew and Adelaide exchanging puzzled looks.

'All we have to do now is find a circus,' Matthew said.

Adelaide shook her head. 'You really *can't* think sideways, can you?'

'What do you mean?'

'Is it too much of a coincidence that a man has disappeared recently from a circus just north of here, and now there's a circus type pretending to recruit children for some evil scheme of his devising? A man who almost certainly murdered his partner in a trapeze act?'

'What was his name again?' Matthew asked as he tried to retrieve his memory of that awful accident under the big top in Hackney.

'I can't remember,' Adelaide admitted, 'but Father almost certainly will. As will the remaining members of his former acrobatic act. They may also be able to tell us where we'd be most likely to find him.'

'But they'll have moved on, surely?' Matthew objected.

'One of the advantages of recently being a candidate for the LCC elections, albeit an unsuccessful one, is that I was obliged to read up on the various services that they conduct for the community. One of those is licensing travelling entertainers like circuses. They may be able to tell us where Baxters' Circus moved on to after Hackney.'

'It's a bit of a long shot, surely?'

'It's better than what we had ten minutes ago,' she reminded him. 'Come on — I'm getting hungry just thinking about the prospect of chasing this swine down before he gets his hands on any more children from this parish that you're supposed to be ministering to. Time for supper, and I don't have time to teach you how to fry pork chops, so this one's my treat.'

'You can get that sort of detailed information from Spring Gardens,' Graham Edmunds told them grumpily from behind the counter in his butcher's shop in Bethnal Green.

'Some snooty clerk in there told us that we'd only get it if we had written authorisation from our elected Council member,' Adelaide told him frostily, 'and because I reside in Hackney, that must be you, even though you appear not to fulfil the residential requirements, if you ever did. We took the precaution of enquiring at the side door, and the lady who answered the door to us in her carpet slippers after coming down the stairs from the rooms above advised us that you do indeed live here in Hare Street, and have done for the past five years or so. It was your brother-in-law's address in Wetherall Road that you used for the benefit of the elections, was it not?'

A light film of sweat broke out on the butcher's forehead beneath the line of his cap, and he swallowed hard before fighting back. 'I know your face, don't I? You're that Suffragist type that was standing against me in the elections, aren't you? Well, now that you and your preacher boyfriend there have managed to interrogate my wife as if we'd committed some dastardly crime, what do you intend to do about it?'

'Nothing — until the next election, anyway — provided that you give us a piece of paper authorising that clerk in Spring Gardens to tell us where Baxters' Circus can be found these days,' Adelaide said.

Edmunds sighed as he wiped his hands on a cloth, ripped a page out of his Order Book, wrote the necessary authorisation out quickly and handed the note to Adelaide.

'So nice to know that our local Councillors are such men of integrity, but I advise you to move accommodation before the next LCC elections. And this man isn't my boyfriend — he's my husband and election agent. Good day to you.'

Collins sighed when advised that he was required to make the return journey through the heavy mid-morning traffic to the West End, and the headquarters of the London County Council, but several church clocks were announcing that it was still only midday as they re-entered the building, where Adelaide haughtily handed over the authorisation and got the details from the same clerk. Advising him that he had an ink stain on his shirt collar, she swept triumphantly from the building with Matthew still in tow, and instructed Collins that their next port of call was the London Hospital.

On the journey back south, Matthew was still expressing the doubts that Adelaide had testily dismissed ever since she'd first raised the proposal. 'For all we know, this missing acrobat chap will be back with his family, and we'll need to start looking elsewhere for this presumed monster who's been enticing the parish children away.'

Adelaide sighed. 'You mentioned that already, and my answer remains the same. If he has returned, then we say nothing about what we know of the death of his mid-air companion, but simply tip off Jennings as to where he may be found. And if he *is* still missing, we get as good of a description of him as we can, then pass it on to Jennings in order to get him located, along — hopefully — with all the missing children, before he has a chance to abuse any more of them.'

'You're expecting a lot of favours from a man you insulted two days ago,' Matthew pointed out.

Adelaide ignored him. 'There's also the point that the young girl Luciana must be well into her pregnancy by now, and I for one would feel happier if Father checked her over, to make sure that she and the child she's expecting are still in good health.'

'All the same, it seems a long way to be travelling on the off-chance.'

'It'll be even further to go if they've settled into their winter quarters in Dorking. But in the belief that they'll drag it out in this place in Lewisham for another couple of weeks for all the last-minute audiences they can attract, it's at least worth the enquiry. We can be there and back in one day, and it's only a question of when Father and yourself can get the day free, and the sooner the better.'

'Are you sure you really want me there?' Matthew asked hopefully.

Adelaide nodded. 'Naturally. That's what husbands do — support their wives. Now stop dithering and think up a few holy words with which to bless the mother-to-be when we find her.'

8

The following Monday, Adelaide gave a little cheer as she looked out of the coach window and saw the caravans ranged around the big top in the centre of Ladywell Fields, in Lewisham. 'See,' she crowed to her father and Matthew, 'it pays to do a little enquiring, and not to take "no" for an answer. Remember the roles that we all agreed to play, and don't get distracted by anything else.'

'I was hoping she'd be less bossy after she married you,' Carlyle grimaced at Matthew as the coach came to a halt, and Edgar Baxter strolled from his caravan to meet them.

It transpired that Adelaide had guessed correctly, and Baxters' Circus was spending an extra two weeks at its final location for the season, mopping up the last of the crowds that were travelling from as far afield as Wimbledon to the west and Chatham in the east. They found the Rossi caravans with ease, and Tarsia Rossi welcomed them and offered to make coffee as they took seats outside.

'You find Giuseppe?' she asked without any obvious enthusiasm.

By prior agreement it was Matthew who spoke for them all. 'Why would we be looking for him?' he asked.

Tarsia spat on the ground. 'He is assassin!' She looked enquiringly at Carlyle. '*Polizia*?'

'I'm not the police,' Carlyle replied. 'I am a doctor, come to examine the girl called Luciana?'

'Come with me.'

Carlyle turned to Adelaide. 'I think she agreed to have her daughter examined. You'd better come with me, to preserve the niceties. I don't want to be accused of improper behaviour in Italian.'

He and Adelaide were shown into one of the caravans, where Luciana was lying on a bed in one corner. It was clearly a residential caravan, and in addition to various items of clothing strewn around the cushioned benches, there was a half consumed meal lying on a table in the centre, and a line of photographs sitting on a sideboard of some sort. Luciana smiled when she saw Adelaide, and spoke to her sleepily in Italian.

Adelaide returned the smile, and indicated her father ("*Medico*") with a hand gesture, and told her — in English — that he was the doctor who had come to check on her baby.

Back outside, Matthew was feeling somewhat left out of things as he sat on the steps of the mother's caravan, an uneasy silence between them.

'Why you not seek Giuseppe? He bad man! You must find him and take him for *appeso*. It is your way here in England, no?'

'What is "*appeso*"?' Matthew asked.

Tarsia placed both hands around her own throat, then made the gesture of something rising up in the air above her head. Matthew had, in his time, officiated as the attendant clergyman at enough judicial hangings to recognise a mime of one when he saw it, and it suddenly occurred to him that his trip down to Lewisham might not be entirely a waste of time after all. He summoned up the simplest words he could manage as he pursued the issue that was clearly of such importance to this woman who, so far as he could tell, was urging him to seek out her own husband for the death penalty.

'Why is Giuseppe bad?' he asked, feeling slightly stupid speaking like a five year old, but Tarsia had picked up his meaning, and responded with another flood of Italian, during the course of which Matthew was able to hear "*corda*", with sufficient hand gestures to suggest that Tarsia was referring to a rope, and "*lardo*", accompanied by a wringing of hands. Since this latter word came close to its English equivalent, and recalling what Carlyle had concluded regarding the state of the dead man's hands, Matthew ventured a further question.

'Giuseppe had "*lardo*" on his hands when catching Roberto?' He accompanied this with a gesture that he hoped indicated the coming together of hands that swiftly parted again.

Tarsia rose to her feet and climbed the steps into her caravan. As she did so, the door to it that had been fully open swung inwards slightly in the fresh breeze, revealing on its front what looked like some advertising poster of the Rossi family in their circus costumes. Matthew was gazing at this, an idea forming in his mind, when Tarsia reappeared carrying several items that she laid down on the grass between them.

She rattled off a mixture of English and Italian that Matthew was just able to follow to a tentative conclusion as she spoke.

'This — Giuseppe wear for act,' she indicated as she held up a large red and green tunic of the sort that Matthew recalled the entire family wearing during the performance he had watched that had ended in Roberto's tragic and fatal fall into the sawdust. Then she held out a small string bag that she opened in order to allow Matthew to look inside. It appeared to contain a powder of some sort, that Tarsia named, '*Borotalco*? For hands?'

She opened a small tin and stuck it under Matthew's nose. He inhaled, then transferred his attention to the bag and did the same. The two powders were clearly identical, to judge by the smell, but he was none the wiser until Tarsia reached down to the grass that was still slightly damp from that morning's dew. She smeared her hand with moisture, then took a handful of the powder in her hand and held it out to Matthew, to show how the powder had absorbed the liquid and left her hand dry. Then she added, 'Giuseppe — all we — do like for act.'

He finally appreciated the point that she was trying to make, and with a broad smile he tried to convey his understanding in simple words. 'Before act — all of you use this for drying hands?'

Tarsia nodded enthusiastically.

'So you rub your hands in it so as to keep a dry grip on the equipment — sorry, the things that you use in the act?'

'Yes, every act,' Tarsia confirmed with a nod. 'You see, look.' She reached down to the grass and lifted up the performance tunic, which to judge by its size would have been worn by a man. To confirm the point she pointed to it and said, 'Giuseppe, he wearing this when Roberto he die.'

'And?' Matthew asked, still at a slight loss to understand where the conversation was heading. Tarsia gave a grimace of triumph as she reached into the side pocket of the tunic and extracted a small flat packet that even Matthew recognised as a proprietary brand of cooking lard. Her eyes flashing with anger, Tarsia made her final point. 'Giuseppe he no have *borotalco* on hand when he go capture Roberto. He have *questo*!'

'So, Giuseppe rubbed his hands in this lard, so that Roberto would slip?' Matthew suggested, and underlined his point by indicating the lard packet then pointing to his own hands.

Tarsia gave a shout of triumph. 'Yes! You clever man!'

Matthew thought quickly about how Carlyle, in his scientific and logical way, might handle this latest information, and a sudden thought struck him. Very gingerly he opened up the remains of the lard wrapper, and found what he had hoped to find. There, in the remains of the lard, was a perfect set of finger impressions. He looked back at Tarsia, before gesturing towards the three items she had retrieved from her caravan. 'I may take these? To find Giuseppe? Then he will hang for murdering Roberto?'

'You bring *polizia* — Giuseppe he get *appeso*?'

'Yes,' Matthew assured her.

She handed over the items to Matthew, then kissed him on each cheek in turn before disappearing back into the caravan, from which the smell of fresh coffee soon wafted out along with the joyful rendition of some sort of Italian folksong rendered in a somewhat shaky contralto voice.

Back in Luciana's caravan, Carlyle had finished examining the pregnant girl and narrating his findings to Adelaide. 'Probably four months, going into five. The child has quickened and is properly positioned for its age. Breasts tender to the touch, with deepened reddening around the areola section of the nipples. Patient reports ongoing nausea and increased urination, along with heightened emotional reaction. At least, I think that's what she was trying to tell me.' He looked up and saw a tear rolling down Adelaide's face. 'What's the problem?' he asked anxiously. 'Did you spot something that I didn't?'

'No,' Adelaide reassured him. 'It's just so — well, so *beautiful*, that's all. A new life forming inside the body of a young woman. I think I might like to study midwifery.'

'Very messy and noisy, in my experience,' her father replied brusquely. 'Stick to pathology — you get less complaints from patients that way.'

'Is baby good?' Luciana asked as she began to put her clothes back on with assistance from Adelaide.

Carlyle nodded.

'Good strong?' Luciana asked hopefully.

Adelaide nodded. 'Good strong,' she confirmed. Then remembering how she herself had turned out looking like a small version of her own mother, she asked, 'You good strong when little?'

'When little, very strong,' Luciana replied. She pointed to the sideboard, on which was displayed an assortment of photographs, then guided Adelaide's hand along them until it came to rest on a curious, and somewhat yellowing and faded picture of a narrow street in what looked like an Italian village. A strange-looking group of individuals appeared to be standing on each other's shoulders, and Luciana called out, 'Me on top!'

Adelaide looked more closely, and could just make out a small girl with a mop of black hair at the very apex of what appeared to be a human triangle. Luciana walked over to stand beside Adelaide and began to point to those in the photograph and name them in turn.

'At bottom — my father Giuseppe and my uncle Davide. And Angelo Sparzese — he dead some time. Then my mother Tarsia and my aunt Anna. Then on top, me. This in Genoa, many times ago. We get much money.'

Carlyle had been too busy putting items back in his medical bag to pay much attention to the conversation that the two women had been conducting, but he froze when he saw the photograph that they were examining. 'Adelaide!' he called urgently. 'Ask the girl what's going on in that photograph!'

'She already told me, Father,' Adelaide replied. 'So far as I can make out, that's her on the top of that human pile, when she was a small girl. It was a family act, apparently, and that's her father and uncle on the bottom row, with her mother and aunt in the middle.'

'A human triangle!' Carlyle muttered, almost to himself. 'Ask how old she was when she first got hauled up there to the top.'

Adelaide smiled at Luciana, pointed to her image at the top of the human triangle, and said, 'Luciana, how old? How many years?'

'*Otto anni.*'

'*Otto*?' Adelaide replied.

'It sounds a lot like "octo",' Carlyle said, 'which is the Latin for eight, so try that on your fingers.'

Adelaide did as instructed, and when she reached eight Luciana nodded. 'Yes! *Otto.* I was not big — not hard of lifting.'

Carlyle whistled softly. 'I think that a bright light just dawned in my head. I'll just write out a note for this delightful young lady to take to the nearest chemist's shop to ease her ongoing nausea, and then we must get back outside to Matthew and rejoin Collins for the journey home. This has been a most fruitful excursion. Could you please do what you can to educate our patient about the importance of visiting a chemist and asking for what I've written down here? She must take two spoonfuls before eating any meal. Good luck with the translation, and I'll meet you outside.'

By the time that Adelaide made it back outside, with a very grateful Luciana in tow, Matthew was talking animatedly to her father, and waving an acrobat's costume about in front of him. She couldn't help herself as she walked up to him with a lopsided grin. 'It'll go very nicely with your dog collar. Will you be wearing it for Evensong, or have the Rossi family acquired the services of a flying priest pretending to wend his way to Heaven?'

'Very droll, I don't think,' Matthew replied with a grin, 'but wait until your father tells you what I found in the pocket.'

'A signed confession by Rossi?' she challenged him.

'As good as,' Carlyle replied, refusing to have his jubilation suppressed. 'With what we've got here, and with a bit of assistance from some zinc powder, we can prove that he murdered his partner in the family act. We'll need the testimony of these ladies, of course, and they'll almost certainly need the services of an interpreter, but it all adds up to a very strong case against Giuseppe.'

'You go chase Giuseppe?' Tarsia Rossi asked.

Carlyle nodded.

'He call name "George Ross" sometimes,' Tarsia added helpfully.

'We'll remember that,' Matthew assured her, 'and we'll let you know as soon as we catch him. May we borrow this photograph from your door? Which one is Giuseppe?'

'*Lui*,' Tarsia replied as she pointed to the brawny bearded man to the front of the group and spat on the ground. 'You go find!'

'Leave it to us,' Matthew assured her, as he unpinned the photograph from the board nailed to the caravan door.

'My, my, I don't think I've ever seen you so galvanised into action,' Adelaide declared as she kissed him lightly on the lips. 'Being a man of action makes you even more attractive.'

Luciana gave a sharp intake of breath, and said something to her mother and aunt.

Tarsia laughed. 'She say priest not for kissing.'

'This one is,' Adelaide replied, 'since he's my husband.'

9

'The message was a bit garbled,' Jennings complained as the mortuary door was opened for him by Adelaide, and he walked in, followed by another man. 'I brought the photographer as requested, and I gathered that it has something to do with your missing children.'

'Among other things, yes,' Carlyle replied with a wry smile. 'We believe that we can now connect them with that murder at the circus that you blankly refused to do anything about.'

'They've moved on, surely?' Jennings objected.

Carlyle nodded. 'Indeed they have, but we tracked them down to their latest location in Surrey, and we brought back some interesting items of evidence, plus what may be the solution to your Spring Heeled Jack problem. I take it that it hasn't gone away?'

'It's got worse,' Jennings grumbled, 'so anything that you can give me on that account will be gratefully received.'

'First things first,' Carlyle said. 'You recall that during that business involving a man who was supposed to have been hanged, but who finished up murdered a full eight months later, we made a breakthrough in photographing finger impressions?'

'I'm obviously not about to forget that — is that why you wanted Jenkins here?'

'Indeed it is, and I'd be grateful if he'd take a clear likeness of this lump of lard with the obvious finger impressions that we've highlighted with zinc powder.'

'Do as he requests, Jenkins,' Jennings told the man with him, 'then perhaps he may grace us with an explanation of what this is all about.'

The camera was set up immediately in front of the bench on which Adelaide carefully erected a tripod, on which she placed a board, to which she then affixed the almost empty lard packet, which was now displaying a set of fingerprints highlighted in grey-blue powder. Several flashes later, both she and her father smiled, and Adelaide set about making tea.

'So whose impressions are they?' Jennings eventually asked.

'The missing acrobat who murdered his partner when he failed to catch him on the trapeze,' Carlyle replied. 'He was supposed to immerse his hands in some sort of powder in order to ensure that they were bone dry when the victim grabbed for them. Instead, he had this almost empty packet of lard in his tunic pocket, and he smeared his hands with it before the deceased took the fatal leap. You'll recall that we found traces of lard on the hands of the corpse when we examined it? Well, Adelaide has done the comparison tests, and it's the same lard that you see in the packet, with the finger impressions of the man who almost certainly smeared his hands with it at the crucial moment. He would of course have left that until he had safely climbed the access rope and only seconds before he did the clever bit, wrapping his feet around the bar of his own trapeze and hanging there, inviting his victim to jump.'

'How do you know that this lard was hidden inside his tunic?' Jennings asked.

'His wife found it in there after he abandoned it, presumably before climbing into his ordinary clothes in order to make good his escape. She was very keen to tell us about it — although her English is somewhat lacking — and you'll find that she's also very eager to see her husband on the end of another rope altogether.'

'But you're no nearer to locating this man?' Jennings stated.

'Yes and no — that's where the link is between this man, who's probably calling himself "George Ross", but who will be easily identified because of his poor spoken English — and the missing children, who at a guess are also your Spring Heeled Jack.'

'Now you've completely bamboozled me,' Jennings admitted as he accepted the mug of tea from Adelaide with a grateful smile.

Carlyle opened a drawer to the side bench and extracted the photograph of Luciana Rossi as a young girl in a village somewhere outside Genoa. 'What do you see in that photograph, Inspector?' Carlyle asked with a self-satisfied smirk.

Jennings glanced at it and replied, 'A bunch of people practising acrobatics, so what?'

'Take a look at the young girl at the top,' Carlyle instructed him. 'That's Luciana Rossi, aged eight at the time, and bottom left is the man we're after — her father, Giuseppe, now probably calling himself "George", wherever he might be found.'

'So?'

'How far off the ground would you say that the girl is?' Carlyle prompted him.

Jennings studied the photograph for a moment, then replied, 'To judge by the height of the house they're standing next to, I'd say ten or twelve feet, why?'

Carlyle clucked dismissively. 'If the house in question had an open upstairs window, the girl could have climbed through it, could she not?'

'Obviously, but … oh, wait a minute, I follow you now.'

'I always find that it's best to let my students come to their own logical conclusions,' Carlyle said condescendingly.

'So you reckon that these burglaries have been committed by a bunch of acrobats doing pyramid impersonations, is that it? If so, isn't that something that might get noticed? I mean, a bunch of people doing fancy tricks wouldn't go unnoticed, even at night, and even in Limehouse, where the weirdest things can be seen even in broad daylight.'

'Supposing they were covered, with, say, a long black cloak?' Carlyle persisted.

Jennings snorted. 'Let's assume that they were doused in invisibility powder while we're at it, shall we?'

Carlyle turned away angrily and took a long sup of his tea while he fought back a suitably offensive riposte, and it was left to Adelaide to pursue the point.

'You just can't be bothered, can you? Let me remind you that there are almost a dozen children missing from the Stepney area, and a dangerous murderer on the loose. We've offered you a strong line of enquiry to follow, but you'd rather sit there and drink tea, raising objections. We believe that this man calling himself "Ross" is holding these poor children captive, and forcing them to commit burglaries by means of an acrobatic trick that's already killed one girl. Or have you forgotten poor little Clarrie Hopgood with the broken legs? Because *I* haven't, and when and if we manage to solve this case — or these cases, rather — I'll make it my business to advise the newspapers of how much assistance we got from the police! Enjoy your tea — I'm going upstairs to supervise yet more Scarlatina bodies being brought down here, and for all the use you are I'll assume that you'll be gone by the time I get back!'

'Once again, you did rather ask for that,' Carlyle commented in the loaded silence that followed the slamming of the door out into the basement corridor.

Jennings looked at Carlyle pleadingly. 'Well, I mean — a "long black cloak" — that's preposterous!'

'Not really,' Carlyle replied. 'My daughter and her husband had occasion to visit a poor grieving lady from their parish whose son is one of those missing. She's become obsessed with the idea that she saw his face outside her bedroom window at dead of night, and that therefore he must be dead. If we begin from the logical starting point that ghosts don't exist, then the only reasonable explanation — however "unreasonable" that may seem to your cynical mind — is that she saw his actual face, and that he's still alive. We then have to ask how his face could have finished up twelve feet or more from road level, and again a physical — as opposed to a metaphysical explanation — is that he was at the top of a human pyramid, just like the girl Luciana in that photograph. Had his mother not woken up, he could have gained entry into the house by way of the bedroom window, like all your other unsolved burglaries.'

'Yes, but...' Jennings began to argue, until Carlyle raised his hand for silence.

'You're about to ask me, are you not, how this lady saw only her son's face, and not the rest of him? That's what Adelaide and Matthew reported her saying, and the most likely explanation I can give you is that he was covered by some dark screen, like a cloak, that not only hid *him* from sight, but those underneath him. As you yourself pointed out, the sight of six or more — and since they were probably only youngsters, make that eight or ten — people in a human triangle would be likely to excite interest even in the early hours of the morning in the centre of Stepney, but if they were covered by some dark cloth, then only the head of the topmost would be visible. At least it's a logical, and more down to earth, explanation then your Spring Heeled Jack alternative.'

'Funnily enough,' Jennings conceded, 'one of the wilder reports we received — which we treated as wildly unlikely at the time, anyway — was that of a human head floating in mid-air. That sounds more like what you're postulating, and I'd certainly be glad to hose down all these wild fantasies about the return of Spring Heeled Jack.'

'I can give you other reasons for discounting that explanation,' Carlyle said knowingly, 'apart from the fact that he'd need to be well into his eighties by now. If you recall, the original Jack spat blue flames, and seemed to be obsessed with making indecent assaults on young servant girls, tearing at their clothing. There have, I assume, been no reports of blue flames during the latest incidents, which have all been about burglary. I suggest to you that we're dealing with a bunch of young people, being held captive by this missing George Ross and being forced to burglarise houses at dead of night by forming a human triangle. The next question has to be "where", does it not? Do you have any likely places to start looking, or have you combed the whole of Limehouse already?'

'Not entirely,' Jennings admitted. 'To be brutally frank with you, Limehouse is the Met's biggest nightmare at the best of times. For a start, a section of it that's technically in Poplar is known, to us anyway, as "The Fenian Barracks", due to the number of disaffected Irish who've gathered there. Even a simple arrest carried out in there is like a military operation, needing a whole platoon of bobbies, occasionally with support from a Guards regiment armed with bayonets. We've had four uniformed bobbies murdered in there in the past year, and the whole area's what we call a "rookery". That's a tightly grouped slum area of closely linked tenements, and the Irish have hit on the idea of drilling through the dividing walls on the top floors. That's produced a sort of long gallery through which men can make their escape when we come calling. So if, for example, we seek to make an arrest at Number 24, the man we're after will escape through to Number 25, or further, simply by climbing into the loft at the top and scuttling down the line.'

'Presumably these are not the houses in which burglaries have occurred?'

'Indeed not, but it may be where these children are being hidden. The houses that have suffered burglaries are located along the better class streets leading north towards Stepney — Salmon Lane, Dixon Street and the like. Many of the householders there own the factories, warehouses and suchlike that are to be found around the Regent's Canal Dockside; they choose not to live too close to the water because of the risk of disease from the Regent's Canal itself.'

'I thought they'd cleaned that up in recent years,' Carlyle observed.

Jennings gave a hollow laugh. 'They pretended to, anyway. As you're no doubt well aware, the Regent's Canal had become the biggest sewer in London — and *that's* saying something, obviously — and the worst section of it was what they call the "Limehouse Basin". That's the portion of it where the canal feeds into the Thames at the Dock. It was once filled with dead bodies, some of them human, and the entire area was so foul that the place where Bow Common Lane passed over it was known as "Stinkhouse Bridge". After a public outcry, they bypassed it with Burdett Road Bridge. No doubt you know better than I do how it was thought for many years that cholera could be caught simply from breathing in the foul air around there.'

'Indeed,' Carlyle confirmed, 'it was known as the "Miasma Theory". But I was one of those who argued that the contagion came from infected water, which is why the clean-up was ordered. Are you saying that it didn't take place?'

'I'm saying that the place is still filthy,' Jennings replied as he screwed up his mouth in distaste. 'You can smell Limehouse Cut from two miles away, and the bobbies cursed with patrols down there find that their uniforms begin to rot with the corruption of the very air. You can smell the men when they come off shift, and their wives are forever complaining about the foul odours they bring into their homes. So, all in all, one can forgive the better off for living well away from there.'

'Presumably there are still factories along the wharves by the Thames exit of the canal?'

'Some, certainly, but they suffer from a financial handicap, in that men can't be induced to work in any of them without getting paid for the danger they're subjecting their health to. Not to mention the social stigma; workers down in Limehouse Basin are called "stinkybums" because of the smell they bring back on their clothing, and a shortage of labourers has led to some of the factories being transferred elsewhere, or closed down altogether. The abandoned buildings have given us other problems, due to the informal and uncontrolled workhouses that have sprung up down there. Unscrupulous folk take in a handful of stray street Arabs, then appeal to the "do-gooding" charity societies for alms to feed and clothe them. The money goes largely on rum and gin, and the poor children finish up worse than they started. At least in the gutter they got to eat occasionally, if only by stealing from street barrows.'

'I'm well aware of how these well-meaning charities are defrauded in that manner,' Carlyle replied frostily, 'since I'm a member of just such an organisation. Come to think of it, that's where I first came across my son-in-law. But from what you're telling me, this George Ross that I've been urging you to locate could have set up his own thieves' kitchen down there, and no-one would regard it as unusual.'

'So do you want me to take some men down there and investigate?' Jennings asked unenthusiastically. 'I won't be popular with the men I select, I can assure you of that.'

'Do what you think best,' Carlyle replied, 'but if we're going to solve two cases for the price of one, it would seem to be the next logical step.'

'I take it that you use "we" in a very general sense,' Jennings scowled under furrowed brows. 'You aren't actually volunteering to come with me?'

'Only if you think that there's a risk that you'll contract some sort of disease down there,' Carlyle replied. 'And even then, that would be best dealt with in here.'

Matthew took a deep breath, reminded himself for the tenth time that it was all for the best, and knocked on the side door to the leather emporium on the High Street. It was opened by Florence Holroyd, covered in flour and with an irritated expression on her face that softened when she realised who was calling. 'Good morning, Reverend West,' she said politely, 'and what can I do for you?'

'I was wondering if I might have a few words with Edgar,' Matthew told her as diplomatically as he could.

She bristled slightly as she asked, 'Is it something to do with his recent attendance at your Junior Bible Classes? He assures us that he's benefitting from them, but lately he's proved to be such an unreliable child — ever since he fell in with that dreadful Tommy Tideswell, not to mention Clarrie Hopgood, who got herself killed.'

'It's actually in connection with Edgar's friends,' Matthew told her. 'As you know, quite a few of them are still missing from the parish, and I was hoping that Edgar would be prepared to give me some more information about where he was while he was missing for those weeks.'

'I'd rather that he forget the whole business,' Florence replied stiffly, 'since he was clearly in bad company, which he assures his father and myself that he's now foresworn, and hopefully his attendance at Bible Classes marks the turning of a corner in his life.'

'God grant that this is the case,' Matthew replied in his best pious tone, 'but the fact remains that we must concern ourselves regarding the safety of those children who are still missing. Anything that Edgar can tell us would be most efficacious in that regard.'

Conscious of the fact that he was beginning to sound like one of his Sunday sermons, Matthew allowed himself to be led up the narrow staircase into the kitchen at the head of it, where Florence invited him to take a seat.

'I'll just get Edgar from his room,' she offered, 'and then I'll get his father to join us, since I'm sure that he'll be as anxious as you to hear what Edgar has to tell us. You know my husband Thomas, of course, since he's one of your sidesmen. A most uplifting sermon last Sunday morning, by the way, considering that it was your first at St Dunstan's.'

'Thank you,' Matthew replied with a beaming smile. 'But it might be better if Edgar's father isn't disturbed in his work downstairs. And, of course, Edgar might be more inclined to tell us the truth if his father's not listening.'

'Are you implying that my son tells lies?' Florence bristled. 'I'm *definitely* calling his father up here, and don't you dare ask a single question of Edgar until he's joined us.'

Matthew sighed at the inevitable, and it was some minutes before they were all round the table, where an apprehensive-looking Edgar couldn't seem to raise his gaze above the surface of the kitchen table.

'Edgar,' Matthew began as gently as he could, 'when we first found you lying in the churchyard, and took you indoors and made you better, you told us that you were too frightened to reveal where you'd been for the previous two weeks or so because of a man who would kill you if you did. Remember?'

'I wasn't feeling at my best,' Edgar hedged, 'and I was probably rambling a bit in my mind. That's what Father suggested, anyway.'

Matthew shot Thomas Holroyd an enquiring look. 'Is that what you suggested to Edgar?'

'No,' Thomas replied, in obvious discomfort. 'I asked him where he'd been, as you can understand, and when he said he couldn't remember anything apart from some man threatening to kill him, I *did* suggest that it might be some sort of nightmare, just to put the boy at ease, you understand.'

'And Edgar wouldn't associate with people like that anyway,' Mrs Holroyd objected.

Matthew swallowed his feeling of frustration and tried again. 'The reason why I'm asking, Edgar, is that your friends — the others who're still with this man — may need to be rescued by the police. The problem with that is that we don't know where they are.'

'Down by the Regent's Canal,' Edgar murmured under his breath, before looking up apprehensively at his parents. 'I know you told me to stay away from there, but Tommy

Tideswell told Clarrie and me about this man called George, who had a place down in Limehouse where we could learn circus tricks and earn some money.'

'And did you go down there with him?' Matthew persisted.

Edgar nodded. 'For a while it was great fun, playing on bouncy things and suchlike, but we didn't get fed very much, and when I said I wanted to come home, this George said that I wasn't allowed to leave, and that if I did I'd die.'

'So this George didn't actually threaten to kill you himself?' Matthew asked.

Edgar shook his head, although the furtive look he gave his father under lowered eyelids gave Matthew the distinct impression that the boy was lying.

'So you see,' Florence Holroyd intervened, 'it's not so urgent a matter after all that these children get rescued, is it? They chose to associate with this circus type, and at least Edgar had the intelligence and good breeding to come home when he realised that there was no future in it, and that he was better off here.'

'What circus tricks did this man teach you?' Matthew persevered. 'Did one of them involve you standing on each other's shoulders?' Edgar nodded uncomfortably, but said nothing, so Matthew ploughed on. 'That wasn't in order to entertain people for money, was it?' he insisted. 'It was in order to burgle houses, wasn't it?'

'Are you accusing our son of being a burglar?' Thomas Holroyd exploded. 'This conversation's gone far enough, Reverend! I'll not sit here and have my son accused of such low behaviour, and I can't for one moment believe such nonsense. "Standing on each other's shoulders?" Have you taken leave of your wits, man?'

'That's how Clarrie Hopgood came to be killed.' Matthew turned to Thomas with anger in his face. 'We believe she fell off the top row during some sort of practice. Either that or she was pushed.'

'So now you're accusing my son of murder as well, are you?' Thomas yelled, red in the face himself. 'Get out of my house — now!'

Matthew could see little point in attempting to get further information out of Edgar, who had in any case all but confirmed his worst suspicions, if only by not disagreeing with some of the more important parts of the picture that was building up. There *had* been a man named George, he *had* enticed children away with a promise of circus training, and it *had* involved learning how to form a human pyramid. Edgar had been lucky to suffer nothing worse than pneumonia, no doubt because he was being held in cold and wet conditions, but it was obvious that he was more intent on avoiding confrontation with his parents than he was on disclosing more information. Matthew did as demanded, and the side door to the street banged angrily behind him as Thomas Holroyd slammed it shut.

'At least I can't be accused of doing bugger-all this time,' Jennings chirped as he admitted himself into the mortuary without waiting for the door to be opened for him after his token knock.

Adelaide turned from the water flask sitting above the gas jet on the bench with a cynical, 'Your nose is presumably finely attuned to the smell of tealeaves being ladled into a pot.'

'Not really, but thanks anyway, if there's some going,' Jennings replied with a confident smirk. 'Then I can tell you where I've been for the past few days.'

'Have you found them?' Carlyle asked with a more welcoming smile.

'I believe I may have,' Jennings told them both as he executed a mock bow. 'There's an abandoned furniture warehouse in Oak Lane, on the eastern perimeter of the docks, and on the bank of the canal. It used to belong to "Peebles Soft Furnishings", but they moved out to a more salubrious location in Bow, where their potential customers are more prepared to visit their showrooms. It's been a pain in the proverbial for the local bobbies ever since, with groups of beggars, layabouts, escapees from the justice system and suchlike taking up temporary residence. But about two months ago we received complaints — from a bunch of vagrants, mind you — that they'd been ordered out by this rough-looking cove armed with a massive club of some sort, jabbering away in broken English that he'd just acquired the occupation rights to the place. His physical description matches the one for this "George Ross" fellow, and the next set of complaints we received were about a mob of children running wild in the delivery yard, using it as some sort of playground.'

'That fits the general picture, certainly,' Carlyle conceded, but Jennings hadn't finished.

'Nothing particularly unusual about children playing down by the Limehouse Cut, but this lot seemed to have unusual play equipment, and very specific games. Some of them were bouncing around on some sort of spring-loaded device, jumping into the air and performing somersaults, while others were juggling with balls and clubs. There've been several break-ins to toy shops, sporting suppliers and the like in the East End during the same period, so we figure that this is where their playthings came from. Apart from your interest in missing children from Stepney, we'd have to investigate anyway, in the hope of recovering stolen goods. Then there are the ghost stories.'

Carlyle sighed heavily. 'Why is it that people can't report simple incidents without giving them supernatural overtones? What could be the remotest bit "ghostly" about a bunch of children playing in a warehouse forecourt, for Heaven's sake?'

'It's not those,' Jennings explained. 'People passing by there at night have reported the eerie sounds of children's voices in the darkness, when there's nothing to be seen. Seemingly the voices move around, then progress down nearby streets, still allegedly invisible, except that from time to time the ghostly image of a child's disembodied face can be seen.'

'That's just what Mrs Vane saw!' Adelaide reminded them both. 'Father was right — they're using a black cloak to hide their movements, with a child at the top of a human pyramid acting as a guide to where to put their feet.'

'Unlikely, the way you describe it,' Carlyle corrected her. 'It's more likely that they creep down the street as individuals, carrying the cloak over their heads like the top of one of those Roman shield devices, then form the pyramid immediately before they reach their intended victim's house. Then the cloak gets passed upwards between them until it's covering all but the top child's head.'

'Whatever way it's being done,' Jennings chimed in, 'I thought that you should learn about it without delay, before my men bust the place and start rounding up the little Arabs.'

'I'm glad you came to us before you did anything of the sort,' Adelaide replied disapprovingly. 'Those are children, remember. Children who in the main are from good homes. They were enticed away by an evil man, and the poor mites probably believed that they were about to realise a dream of joining the circus. Then they became captives of this brute who was fierce enough in his methods and manner to scare away the riff-raff who were already occupying that warehouse. Imagine how tough and intimidating he must seem to a group of scared young children with little to no experience of the less lawful parts of the East End. You must treat those children as victims, Inspector — not simply barge in there and start battering their skulls with your billy clubs.'

'Adelaide has a very good, if somewhat exaggerated, point,' Carlyle agreed. 'We already know of one child — the Hopgood girl — who died while in that awful man's company. We don't know how precisely she came to have those broken legs, but we can't rule out direct violence from the man Rossi. There may be other children in there with injuries, and I must insist on coming with you and your men when you finally kick the doors down.'

'And that includes me,' Adelaide insisted. 'Not to mention my husband, since if these children are who we think they are, then they're from his parish, and some of them will be less likely to panic and run away in all directions if they see him in the company of your bobbies.'

'When did you have in mind?' Jennings asked, with no indication that he found their demands unreasonable. 'I'll need at least a day to borrow the men I'll need from various parts of the Met, and you'll need to get the Reverend.'

'I'll need to enquire when he'll be free, although I imagine that he'll be prepared to give this matter some priority,' Adelaide assured him.

'Did it not occur to either of you two that I might have other calls on my time as well?' Carlyle asked grumpily. 'Even if you can perform a miracle and keep London crime-free for twenty-four hours, my slab will still be occupied by uncertain cases from the hospital wards above where we're currently standing, calmly contemplating the absence of any mortuary services for as long as it takes. I have a deputy of sorts, but Dr Morton can be a bit unreliable under pressure. I deliberately avoided using the phrase "cutting corners", as I hope you appreciated.'

'Clearly we'll need another meeting anyway,' Jennings pointed out, 'if only in order to agree how the operation will be carried out. Can we make that either tomorrow or the day after?'

'Since today's Friday, and tomorrow might be a bit short notice,' Adelaide pointed out. 'It'll clearly have to be Monday. I assume I don't have to explain why Sunday's out for Matthew. He's taking the morning service again this week, but he's usually exhausted for the rest of Sunday when he does that, so Monday suggests itself. I'm happy to offer our house as the meeting place, and I'll prepare us all some supper.'

Carlyle beamed. 'If nothing else comes of this, at least I'll be enjoying my daughter's cooking again.'

10

Matthew's heart swelled with pride as usual as he looked down at his larger than ever Sunday morning congregation. He could, had he been so vain, have concluded that the reason for the large attendance was the drawing capacity of his homely sermons, but the reality was that Christmas was only weeks away, and something about the impending celebration of the birth of the Saviour seemed to bring out the religious fervour in the local community, so that the congregations tended to swell in size towards the middle of November and into the early weeks of December.

He concluded his sermon with the traditional 'Praise be', then moved to his place before the altar to announce the 'collect' hymn. It was 'Abide with me', a particularly lengthy one at the best of times, but guaranteed to be even longer at the almost funereal pace that organist Mabel Carter played it. It was a popular one for engaging the congregation while the collection plates were being passed down the rows of pews by sidesmen Thomas Holroyd and Ernest Sharman. They were taken immediately thereafter into the vestry to be counted, prior to the total being placed in the strongbox fixed to the wall, for which Matthew had the only immediately available key, kept securely in the pocket of his surplice. The spare key was traditionally kept in a safe alternative place by the curate, and in Matthew's case it was his desk drawer at home.

Due to the sheer size of that day's congregation, the collection took a little longer than usual, and the congregation were approaching the end of the penultimate verse as Matthew accompanied the two sidesmen into the vestry with the burgeoning collection plates they were carrying. The atmosphere between Matthew and Tom Holroyd had been somewhat chilled ever since Matthew had been ordered from the Holroyd house, but there was no time for idle chit-chat anyway. Matthew needed to be back out in front of the altar for the benediction prayer once the hymn finished, prior to the congregation filing back out into the shelter of the front porch, on which a light sleet had been falling an hour previously.

'Just count it between you, then put it all in the strongbox,' Matthew instructed the two sidesmen as he reached into his surplice. 'Here's the key — I need to get back in there.'

The service came to a close, and Matthew moved swiftly outside to thank his parishioners for their attendance. Even Mrs Holroyd, who could barely manage to mutter a response, and when she did it was inaudible. It occurred to Matthew that this was perhaps as well in the circumstances.

It was the following morning before Matthew woke up with a start and realised that he hadn't retrieved the key to the vestry strongbox from Holroyd and Sharman. If it came to that, he would need to enter the amount of the collection into the parish financial record, so would need to retrieve what he hoped was some sort of note of the total left for him in the vestry by his two sidesmen the previous day. Since it was not the practice at St Dunstan's to take a collection during Evensong, which had been conducted yesterday by the vicar, the amount collected at the morning services was an important component of the 'Poor Fund' that the parish maintained for those of their faithful who fell upon hard times.

Once inside the vestry, he cursed his own forgetfulness when he realised that in his hurry to get over here after breakfast, after Adelaide had left for the hospital, he'd left the spare key at home, along with the book in which the total had to be recorded.

He lifted the piece of paper from the table, and noted with a deep sense of satisfaction that the previous morning's total had been marginally over seventeen pounds, all of it presumably safely locked inside the strongbox in the wall. Humming happily to himself, he closed the vestry door behind him and began to walk through the chancel and past the altar on his way back towards the nave.

He stopped when he saw something unusual lying on top of the altar. A small drawstring bag of the sort used by street market traders, and it looked to be full of something or other. He walked over, picked it up and shook it enquiringly. It came as no surprise to him that it jingled loudly, and his curiosity was instantly aroused.

With a stab of alarm he walked quickly back into the vestry and checked the door to the strongbox, then heaved a sigh of relief when he confirmed that it was indeed locked, and presumably had been since the previous morning's service. The bag of money that had mysteriously appeared on the altar would nevertheless have to be accounted for, and he couldn't do that until he went home for the spare key, opened up the strongbox and compared the amount in there with the amount on the note left by Tom Holroyd. In any case, if someone had been stealing collection money, why would they be so careless as to leave their ill-gotten gains sitting on the altar? A sudden fit of conscience?

His mind fully occupied as he left the vestry for the second time, Matthew pulled up with a start when he saw a woman standing by the third row of the nave, staring at him and looking a little confused, or perhaps guilty.

'Sorry, Reverend,' Mrs Holroyd said as she looked up at him. 'Only I left my brolly in my pew yesterday morning, and I've only just had time to come in and get it back. I got properly soaked on my way home yesterday, and I should by rights have come back in for it then, but I was anxious to get dinner on for my family — so, here I am. Hope that's in order?'

'Yes, of course,' Matthew assured her, grateful, if a little puzzled, that she seemed to have returned to speaking to him in a civil manner. 'The church is open to all, at all times, as you're well aware. How's Edgar recovering from his ordeal?'

'Almost back to normal. But not in any state to answer any more of your questions, if that's what you're really asking,' she added sharply. 'And so good day to you.'

'An excellent shepherd's pie!' Jennings enthused as he helped himself to more from the bowl in the centre of the supper table. 'Do I detect the addition of parsley?'

'Very well spotted,' Adelaide said. 'I always find that it helps to spice up what might otherwise be a bland meal. And nothing is potentially more bland than minced beef and mashed potato, even with carrots and peas mixed in before the final bake. Yet it's ridiculously simple to make. So simple, in fact, that Matthew made this one — under my supervision, of course.'

Matthew went slightly red. 'My mother always insisted on doing all the cooking at home, and since I have a younger sister, she got the cookery lessons while my brother and I just had to eat the consequences.'

'All very touching,' Carlyle commented with light sarcasm, 'but we're not here to learn of Matthew's progression up the domesticity ladder.'

'No, indeed not,' Jennings agreed. 'In the absence of any alternative, I suggest tomorrow evening, at around seven p.m. It'll be dark by then, and I'm advised that it's a new moon phase, so we'll have the advantage of a blackened approach before we storm the place.'

'I don't like the sound of that,' Matthew broke in. 'We're dealing with children here, not armed footpads or bullion train robbers.'

'All the same, my men will be going in with loaded firearms, just in case,' Jennings insisted. 'The man in command of these children may well be armed himself, and from what we've learned about him he's a very dangerous character.'

'Then you can count me out,' Carlyle announced loudly and firmly. 'If any guns go off, intentionally or otherwise, the children are likely to panic and get caught in any crossfire. I don't wish to be prising bullets from the bodies of dead youngsters.'

'And I won't be there either, for largely the same reasons,' Matthew chimed in. 'My role in life is to preserve souls, particularly young ones, and I couldn't contemplate for one moment being a party to the sort of police "raid" that you're planning.'

'If my father and husband both feel like that, then you know my answer,' Adelaide added.

Jennings shook his head in exasperation. 'Are you suggesting that we send them a written notice of our intention to call on them — perhaps leave our calling card the previous day?'

'Obviously not,' Carlyle replied curtly. 'We're just saying that this has got to be organised differently from a "take down" of some Chinese pipe house. I suggest that Matthew and I enter softly at first, with a handful of your officers — armed, if they must be, to ensure our protection against "Mr Ross", should he prove to be there. We explain quietly why we're there, and that we have enough men outside to ensure their safety, then we invite them to accompany us back to Stepney. Some of them may be too ill, injured, or under-nourished, to walk back, and the weather may prove to be inclement, so perhaps you might consider having a few police coaches in attendance to convey them to their homes.'

'Do you want a brass band playing hymns as well?' Jennings demanded sarcastically.

'Of course not,' Carlyle replied testily. 'It's simply a matter of ensuring that the children are not exposed to anything too frightening for them. From what we know already it seems highly likely that they're already terrified of Ross. The last thing we need is a whole contingent of armed police officers barging in there with loaded firearms. Those are our terms, anyway — either this is done peacefully, or the three of us don't wish to be involved.'

Jennings gave a hollow laugh. 'It may be more "peaceful" than you imagine, Doctor. The latest reports from the neighbours are that the place has suddenly gone very quiet. There's no sign of the children playing in the delivery yard, and very little noise from inside. Simply the odd wail or groan, which of course have become exaggerated accounts of "ghost children" occupying a haunted warehouse. It may be that when we do go in there, we'll only have the spirits of dead children to confront.'

'Horrible!' Adelaide whispered as she sought Matthew's protective arms.

Matthew registered his protest. 'This is not a suitable subject for a twisted comment such as that, Inspector. And if there is some reason why the children are distressed, then the sooner we get in there and rescue them, the better.'

'Then let's make it tomorrow evening — seven p.m., in Oak Lane, outside the delivery yard of the old Peebles Factory. My men are getting tired of sitting around doing nothing while they wait for the command to move in on the place. Or do you still have scruples?'

'Yes, we do,' Carlyle told him, 'but this evening's conversation has only made me even more concerned for the welfare of these captive children if we're not there to moderate your tactics. So tomorrow at seven it is.'

The following morning, Matthew was seated in his study at home, counting the money from the bag he'd found on the altar, when there came an imperious knock on his front door. He sighed, rose from his desk, and walked down the hallway to open it. There, looking as if his world had just come to an end, was the vicar, Joseph Mulholland.

'May I come in, Matthew?' he asked solemnly.

Matthew led the way down to his study, and invited Mulholland to take a seat. The vicar's eyes lit upon the coins, and the occasional banknote, strewn across the desk, and asked, 'Where did that money come from, Matthew?'

'Inside the church,' Matthew replied. 'It had been left in a bag on the altar, and my first thought was that it might have been stolen from Sunday's collection. I've just finished counting it, then I'm off to check the contents of the strongbox in the vestry against the total that Tom Holroyd counted on the morning. It should be somewhere around seventeen pounds.'

'Seventeen pounds, four shillings and sixpence, to be precise,' Mulholland replied darkly. 'Tom Holroyd has a good memory for figures, given his commercial acumen, and that was the sum he mentioned to me when he called in to see me yesterday evening.'

'And why would he do that?' Matthew asked.

'Before I tell you that, how much is there on your desk?' Mulholland asked.

Matthew glanced down at the paper on which he'd written the amount. 'It comes to seven pounds and one shilling, almost all of it in coins, as you can see.'

Mulholland's face fell even further as he extracted a piece of paper of his own from his waistcoat pocket, and read out the figures written on it. 'There was only ten pounds three shillings and sixpence in the strongbox when I checked it earlier, using an extra key that we had cut when the box was first installed, and of which you weren't aware. That means that there's seven pounds and one shilling missing — precisely the amount that you have there.'

'I was right, then,' Matthew confirmed with a smile. 'This money that I found on the altar must have been stolen from the Sunday collection. But how did you come to have a copy of the totals calculated by the sidesmen?'

'Tom Holroyd contacted me, very embarrassed by what he suspected had been a theft from the collection plate. But stolen by who, exactly?' Mulholland added ominously. 'And why would someone go to the trouble of stealing money, only to leave it lying on the altar? An unlikely tale, you'd have to agree.'

'It's not a tale,' Matthew insisted as an uneasy feeling began to creep into his mind. 'I found it on the altar, and brought it back here to count it, in the same belief as yours, namely that it might have been stolen. But what led to Holroyd's suspicion?'

'His wife advised him that she saw you leaving the vestry with what looked and sounded like a bag of coins. She was in the church retrieving an abandoned umbrella, apparently. But she said nothing about the money being on the altar, from what Holroyd advises me.'

'That's because I went back into the vestry in order to check whether the strongbox was still locked, as indeed it was,' Matthew explained. 'I'd already left the vestry the first time, on my way out of the church, when I first found the money on the altar.'

'And why were you there in the first place?' Mulholland demanded with a piercing look.

Matthew could sense the moral ground slipping away from him as he told the truth. 'I went into the vestry the first time in order to check the total from the collection and enter it into the record book. Then I realised that I'd forgotten to take over both the strongbox key and the record book, so I set off back here to get them, and that's when I found the money bag on the altar.'

Mulholland remained silent for a long moment, then looked back at Matthew with a sad frown. 'You'll appreciate that I can only proceed on the basis of the facts that are in my possession. I can hardly doubt the words of two such respected parishioners as the Holroyds, and what they tell me raises at least an initial suspicion against you.'

'You must be well aware that the Holroyds bear me a grudge after I tried to get information from their son Edgar regarding the whereabouts of the missing children,' Matthew pointed out, wishing that his face hadn't flushed with what would no doubt look like guilt. 'And what about the "respect" that you owe to me, as your curate?'

'I'm sorry, Matthew,' Mulholland said sadly. 'If you know your Classics, then you'll be familiar with the line that "Caesar's wife must be above suspicion". I cannot be seen to do nothing, out of favouritism to you, while this suspicion hangs over your head.'

'What are you saying? And what suspicion, exactly? Surely not stealing from the collection plate? A paltry seven pounds?'

'You may of course remain in this house while the matter is investigated,' Mulholland continued as if Matthew hadn't spoken. 'But I'm afraid that I have no option but to suspend you from duty.'

When Adelaide returned home in the middle of the afternoon, as arranged, in order to gather together the essentials that they would need for their rescue of the parish children, she found Matthew far from ready. Instead, he sat staring disconsolately at the living room wall, sprawled in his favourite armchair with his long legs sticking out in front of a fire that had gone out because he had been too distracted to keep it going. The house had a gloomy chill to it, but she abandoned her initial rebuke for letting the fire go out when he revealed the reason for his distraction.

'But that's ridiculous!' she protested. 'Also grossly unfair, and probably legally actionable! As if anyone could seriously suspect you of stealing seven pounds from parish funds! It's not as if we need even your entire income, given my independent wealth, so why would you possibly need to pilfer a measly seven pounds?'

'Thank you for reminding me — yet again — that our comfortable lifestyle comes from your investments,' Matthew muttered, seemingly on the verge of tears, and Adelaide threw herself on her knees at his feet.

'I'm *so* sorry, darling! Please forgive me, and don't ever for one moment think that I regard you as some sort of kept consort. I *really* wasn't thinking, and I could bite my tongue off.

It's just that I'm so angry that anyone could think so badly of you, when I know what a wonderful soul you are, and I'm going to go straight up to the Mulhollands' house to give them a piece of my mind!'

'Don't, please!' Matthew begged of her. 'It could only make matters worse, and I'm sure that I'll be able to prove my innocence. I suspect that the hands of the Holroyds are in this somehow. It was too convenient by half how Mrs Holroyd just happened to be in the church to see me walking away with the money bag, and there was no reason why Tom Holroyd should have taken it upon himself to reopen the strongbox in order to find that there was money missing from Sunday's takings. If it comes to that, why did he still have the key? He should have handed it back to me after the service, but I hadn't given that a second thought when I came back home for dinner on Sunday. I was just so pleased at the size of the congregation, and I spent so long under the porch, thanking them for their attendance, that time slipped away from me, and I just hurried back across here when I realised that dinner would already be on the table.'

'You suspect Tom Holroyd of taking the money?' Adelaide asked, still outraged at the injustice being done to the man she loved and admired so much.

Matthew nodded. 'Yes, but he doesn't need the money any more than we do, given the success of his business. I suspect that it's some attempt by the Holroyds to blacken my name, in case we say anything untoward about their son's involvement in the disappearance of the rest of the children. Oh, damn it — what time is it? We need to get ready to meet with Jennings down in Limehouse, don't we?'

Adelaide leaned across his outstretched legs and kissed him warmly. 'There's plenty of time for that, so don't worry. It's only just after three, and Father will be here with the coach at around six-thirty. Sidney Morton's taken over at the mortuary, and Father's gone home to get a few medical supplies organised in his bag. Have you eaten?'

'I couldn't face even the leftovers of that delicious shepherd's pie, after what happened this morning,' Matthew admitted. 'But I could manage a little cheese, if there is any. And a cup of tea, if you're offering.'

11

A church bell somewhere rang out seven times, and Matthew reasoned that it had to be coming from St Mary-le-Bow, to their north-east in Cheapside, given the chill easterly wind that was blowing wastepaper and other detritus around their boots. He, Adelaide and Carlyle stood huddled in the gateway of the rope works on the opposite side of Oak Lane from the disused factory warehouse where, in a few minutes' time, they hoped to find the missing children from Stepney.

It was almost unnaturally dark, and it was easy for Matthew's imagination to play tricks on him as he listened to the eerie sounds that drifted in on the wind. The muttered ramblings of an early evening drunk as he argued with himself on his unsteady route back to some tenement hovel further down the dingy street, the occasional shrill voice of a mother calling for her children, and the distant rumble of carriages.

He started as a harsh whisper jolted him back into reality, and the cheery face of Inspector Jennings appeared from inside the gateway. He chuckled. 'Got you that time, didn't I? You all look as if you'd seen a ghost!'

'I'll turn you *into* a ghost if you ever pull a trick like that again,' Carlyle admonished him. 'And why are you here alone?'

'You clearly wouldn't last five minutes out here in big bad Dockland,' Jennings crowed, despite Carlyle's threatening tone. 'My men are all around us even as we speak, fully primed and loaded, and ready to go. I just have to blow this whistle.'

'No whistles,' Carlyle insisted. 'I suggest that the four of us move very stealthily across that open space to what appear to be the front doors, then quietly open them and see what confronts us. There's no sound coming from the place that I can make out, and the lights seem to have been extinguished — assuming that they have any — so we may have the advantage of surprise. Do you have any torches available?'

'We've got a heap of those fancy "flambeau" things that we've copied from the Americans,' Jennings replied proudly. 'They're fully primed with paraffin and ready to be lit.'

'Not yet,' Carlyle insisted. 'Let's wait until we're at the door. And keep your men well back to begin with.'

They crossed the road as silently as the darkness permitted, the only sounds behind them being the stealthy tread of boots as Jennings signalled silently for his men to follow behind them. Then they progressed cautiously across the empty yard towards the front doors of the warehouse, Carlyle in the lead, setting the pace, with Matthew, Adelaide and Jennings following closely behind him. They were obliged to steer carefully round various objects they encountered in the pitch darkness that appeared to be abandoned 'play' items such as bats, balls and hoops. At one point Matthew's foot collided with what turned out to be, on closer inspection, a long rectangle of what looked like the skin from a curiously shaped drum that was raised a few inches off the ground on a metal frame. 'What in Heaven's name is that?' he whispered as he nursed his bruised ankle.

It was Jennings who answered. 'I've seen firemen use them to rescue people from burning buildings. They get the person to jump out of their window onto it, and it breaks their fall by bouncing them back up into the air. The fire people call them "life nets".'

'Don't you recall seeing the two Rossi ladies bouncing up and down on them in order to reach their trapezes?' Adelaide reminded him. 'I imagine that Ross was teaching the children how to do acrobatic tricks using these things.'

Carlyle called for total silence as they reached the front doors, and they strained their ears for any indication of what might be taking place inside. All they could make out was some sort of agonised groaning that brought back unsettling recollections of the recent ghost stories that had been circulating regarding the place.

'Right,' Carlyle whispered hoarsely, 'in we go. Inspector, please light us each a torch, then I suggest that Matthew leads the way.'

'Why Matthew?' Adelaide demanded.

'Because he's the tallest,' her father replied, 'and if there are indeed parish children in there, then they might recognise him and remain calm.'

'And what if Ross is waiting for us in there?' Jennings challenged him.

There was a moment's hesitation before Carlyle replied, 'Draw your own firearm if you must, but hold your men back until they're required. Hopefully they won't be.'

The double doors creaked alarmingly as Matthew pushed the door open, a lighted torch held at head height in front of him. He stepped carefully inside and raised the torch, and into dim view came several ghostly pale faces, blinking at the sudden light. Only then did Matthew become aware of a dreadful stench.

'What on earth's that smell?' Jennings demanded, puzzled and nauseated at the same time.

'What do you think?' Carlyle replied in a flat tone that indicated that his thoughts were elsewhere.

'*Shit*, is what I think,' Jennings replied disgustedly. 'And with a side order of spew, if my nose doesn't deceive me.'

'It doesn't,' Carlyle confirmed, 'but to a more sensitive and experienced medical nose, there's something far more alarming. Adelaide, what else can you smell?'

Adelaide hesitated for a moment before replying, 'Some sort of fish?'

Carlyle grunted his agreement. 'Now let's see what you remember from that book on contagious diseases that you were always borrowing from my study. Human excrement with a fishlike odour — does that ring any bells with you?'

'Only … but no, that's been eradicated, surely? No … please God, no … not…?'

Carlyle ordered everyone back outside, then turned to Jennings. 'Keep your men out of there, unless you want to lose most of them. Then form a ring around the place, and don't let anyone in or out.'

'There's no immediate danger, surely?' Jennings argued.

Carlyle replied with a hollow laugh. 'Far more than any of us could have imagined. Unless I'm very much mistaken — and I dearly hope that I am — what lies inside there is as deadly as a bullet, although it takes longer. It's called cholera.'

'Even an ignorant bobby like me knows that cholera's been eradicated in London for the past thirty years or so,' Jennings objected.

Carlyle sighed heavily. 'You told us earlier that we wouldn't last five minutes in your environment, Inspector, so let me now welcome you to mine. Cholera is not some sort of nuisance that you can rid yourself of, like you police officers periodically drive pickpockets off the streets. Cholera is lurking everywhere, waiting for the unwary, and all it needs are the right conditions for it to breed.'

'At a guess, the children in there were taking water from the canal,' Adelaide suggested.

Her father nodded. 'That would also be my best guess.' He turned back to address Jennings. 'Time for a medical history lesson, Inspector. And Matthew might like to take note as well. For many years we thought that cholera was passed on from person to person through their breath — the so-called "Miasma Theory". Then a very skilled, determined and observant doctor called John Snow proved that the contagion was caused by polluted water from a local pump that had been allowed to come into contact with human sewage. He died before he received the recognition he deserved, but when the stink from the Thames flowing under the noses of those in the Parliament buildings in Westminster grew too unbearable, they cleaned up one of the city's most popular water sources, and the reported cases of cholera in suburbs along the river banks dropped to such an extent that the former Metropolitan Board of Works was encouraged to drive sewers under most of the city as it then was.'

'So why is it back amongst us?' Jennings quibbled.

Carlyle waved his hand in the direction of the building they had just left. 'On the far side of that building is the biggest sewer of the lot, according to what I have read, and what you claim can be smelt on any day,' he announced with a sour expression. 'The nature of our political world is such that when some new discovery is made that will benefit the community, it is made available first to those of wealth and privilege, of which of course I am one. There is a flush toilet in my house in Hackney, as there is in almost every other house in that suburb, but no-one around Limehouse can boast of one. They use buckets, and those buckets get tipped into the canal over there.

'The bacteria that constitute the cholera sickness can breed both on, and in, human waste, which is one of the primary ingredients of the water to be found in Limehouse Cut. Even if there was once a water tap installed in these premises behind us that those children were forced to occupy, it would almost certainly have been removed at the request of the factory owners when they moved out, leaving the nearby canal as a tempting source of water for any vagrants taking up residence in the empty premises.

'Even if they did not drink that water, and God alone knows that the smell coming off it would dissuade anyone with normal faculties, they were probably washing themselves with it. The smallest amount entering their mouths accidentally, or through an open cut, would allow the filth to find its target. Once one child was infected, contact with their body fluids by any other child would provide a ready avenue of travel for the infection.'

'It's all too horrible to contemplate, even in cold medical language such as yours,' Adelaide protested with a quivering voice that denoted impending tears.

Matthew held her close to his chest, nuzzling the top of her bonnet with his lips. 'Are they all bound to die?' he asked softly.

Carlyle shook his head. 'Some in there will almost certainly be dead already, I'm afraid, but as for the rest, it will depend upon the strength of their natural constitutions, and what we can do for them.'

'I always thought that there was no cure for cholera,' Jennings said.

'In a strict medical sense, there isn't,' Carlyle told them all. 'It must run its course through the victim, which is unpleasant for both that person and those around them. But if the person's basic constitution is robust enough, and they are kept adequately dosed with liquids and whatever solids they can be enticed to consume, then they will emerge alive from it. Emaciated and filthy, but alive.'

'So what can we do for those poor wretches inside there?' Matthew asked.

'First of all,' Carlyle told them all brusquely, 'we must maintain a rigid regime of non-contact between the inside and the outside. I will clearly have to go in there and do what I can, while Adelaide will hopefully agree to be my assistant. But once we go in there, we cannot come out again, since there is a risk that we will bring the contagion out on our clothing.'

'What about me?' Matthew asked sadly. 'Are you saying that Adelaide and I must be parted for however long this takes?'

'I'm afraid so,' Carlyle confirmed, 'and that also precludes you from coming in to minister to the dead and the dying. God will take whomsoever He chooses, without your advice or assistance. But you will be our link with the outside world, and from time to time Adelaide or myself will come to the door with a list of the things that we need, which must be left for us by the doors. It may well have to be Adelaide who emerges from time to time, but I must emphasise that there must be no physical contact between you when she does.'

'What do you want from me?' Jennings asked.

Carlyle smiled. 'Your priority may well prove to be keeping these two apart, but for the moment you'll be required to access the items that we'll need in there. First of all, a regular supply of fresh water. And I don't mean sending a constable to the nearest tap with a bucket. What you must do is locate an indisputably clean water source, and then fill some sort of container vehicle with it. There are commercial water carriers still in business, I believe, and you must either commission one on a permanent basis, or acquire your own and keep it moving between here and the water source. Once it's delivered here, we can move it inside in buckets, so we'll need a generous supply of those as well. Along with a seemingly endless supply of mops and towels, the precise purpose for which I won't dwell upon. That's just the beginning, along with a generous quantity of clean blankets, sheets and rags. Then I'll need vinegar in almost industrial quantities, in addition to whatever medical supplies I call for, in respect of which I'll supply you with the necessary letter of authorisation signed by me.'

'Do you want me to act as the messenger between here and the Stepney community?' Matthew asked.

'That's something else,' Carlyle replied sharply. 'Until we're in a position to take the survivors home, there must be no mention of what we've discovered here. For one thing, we don't know which of them will survive, but more to the point I don't want this place under siege from parents trying to get in to comfort their offspring, thereby taking cholera back into Stepney.'

'What about my officers back out here?' Jennings asked. 'Do I send them home?'

'Not yet,' Carlyle replied. 'We don't yet know where, if anywhere, in this place we're likely to come up against the elusive Mr Ross, and I want him arrested when and if we do. The other reason is that I need some sort of human barrier around the place, to prevent anyone getting in. Not just desperate parents, but newspaper types as well. If word gets out that we're containing an outbreak of cholera in there, there's likely to be a general panic.'

'And food?' Jennings asked.

Carlyle thought for a moment, then gave him a verbal list. 'Bread, lots of fruit, cooked vegetables, and perhaps a little fish. To begin with we'll simply be keeping up their body liquids, to stop them dehydrating as the cholera rips through their systems, turning everything to smelly water. The need for more solid food will come later, as their systems slowly return to normal, and the priority will then be to build their strength back up.'

Matthew had been keeping the thought to himself, in order not to distress Adelaide further, but sooner or later he had to know, and the moment now seemed right. 'If you do finish up with some deceased in there, what will you do with their bodies?'

Carlyle's face fell as he supplied the answer. 'This is going to sound brutal and uncaring, and I say it with considerable regret, but we're going to have to think in terms of creating some sort of graveyard out here. Inspector, you might wish to bring in some labourers to break up the cobbled surface of this yard, and dig a series of grave holes. Then I'll need you to acquire a considerable quantity of quicklime that can be thrown onto the corpses, then slaked with water. This will effectively prevent any contagion leaching back up through the soil.' He caught the look on Matthew's face, and smiled. 'In due course we might prevail upon the authorities to either sell or lease this portion of land to us, and with your ecclesiastical assistance we can turn it into a memorial garden to which grieving relatives may return in order to pay their respects. Given the straitened circumstances in which we find ourselves, would this be sufficient in the eyes of God, do you think?'

'It's probably the best we can do,' Matthew grimaced, white in the face at the enormity of the task he would face in comforting parents bereft of their precious children.

'Very well, then,' Carlyle concluded in as business-like a tone as he could manage, 'let's set about our various tasks.'

Adelaide looked longingly at Matthew. 'You *do* understand, don't you?'

He kissed her tenderly, and replied, 'If it's what you want to do, and if you think it's for the best, then of course I understand. Just make sure that you keep yourself alive.'

'That's something else,' Carlyle said to Matthew as he turned back one final time. 'Adelaide will need a regular supply of gloves and handkerchiefs, as will I. Nothing too expensive or fashionable, since we'll be burning them after each use. It's just that we're likely to get through a depressingly large number of them.'

'Leave that to me,' Matthew confirmed. 'Will she have time to read, do you think? I can bring her some books from home.'

'Well minded,' Carlyle said as he looked towards Jennings. 'Can you get the gas reconnected in here? I'm assuming that it was cut off when the previous occupants left.'

'That shouldn't present a problem,' Jennings assured him with a curt nod.

'What books do you want?' Matthew asked of Adelaide, but her father beat her to it.

'Find every book you can on the life of a woman called Florence Nightingale. She set the standard for the sort of nursing that's about to be required of Adelaide, and it might serve to inspire her. Now then, young Florence the Second, follow me, and bring that torch.'

As the doors closed heavily behind them, Matthew turned sadly to Jennings. 'At least you have plenty to keep you occupied, with that impossible list of demands from Dr Carlyle. All I have to do is bring back a load of handkerchiefs and gloves, and find a book about some woman I've never heard of.'

'Never heard of Florrie Nightingale?' Jennings replied disbelievingly. 'Where on earth have you been? She's famous for saving the lives of soldiers during Crimea — before my time, of course — and she's set herself up in St. Thomas's Hospital, across the river in Lambeth. They say that she's an inspiration to all women everywhere who want to be doctors and suchlike.'

'So she's a doctor, you say?' Matthew asked, his curiosity tweaked by what sounded like a woman after Adelaide's own heart.

Jennings shrugged. 'Don't know about that, exactly, but she seemingly knows a lot about healing the sick.'

'No wonder Dr Carlyle wanted me to get books about her for Adelaide, although I'm surprised he hasn't got some of his own.'

'Who knows? Maybe he didn't want to encourage his own daughter to go the same way. But talking of things we've got to do, I'd better get these men of mine organised. Can't have them standing around here, stomping their feet against the cold.'

Matthew suddenly realised that he had been shivering against the cold night air himself, and his thoughts went out to Adelaide and her father inside the building. 'It must be freezing in there as well,' he commented with a nod towards the doors. 'Can't we get them some sort of heating while they go about their work?'

Jennings shrugged again, or perhaps he too was shivering from the cold. 'If the doctor's right, and there's gas installed in there, the chances are that there's some sort of heating, as well as light fittings. The sooner I get the gas turned back on, the better.'

'Will the gas people agree to do that, simply on the say-so of the Met?' Matthew asked doubtfully. 'And who's going to pay for it, anyway?'

Jennings snorted. 'The good doctor obviously didn't think that one through, any more than he considered the cost of all the things he demanded, not to mention the side-lining of at least six men at a time, guarding this place.'

'But surely, when you tell your superiors why it's so necessary?'

'You think I'm going to tell them? I can just imagine the reaction of my Chief Inspector when I tell him how much money and manpower I'm proposing that we invest in a few sick children.'

'But how can you get the authority to do all the things that Dr Carlyle requested, and use up so many police constables, without telling him why?'

'That's my problem,' Jennings reminded him, 'and you've got a few of your own to solve, from what I heard. For a start, you have to go about your duties as the curate of a busy parish without letting on that you're spending most of your days down here, acting as go-between for a bunch of the parish children who're dying of cholera.'

'That won't be so much of a problem as it might have been, funnily enough,' Matthew told him. 'I'm currently suspended from duty anyway.'

'What did you do — thump the vicar?'

'None of your business,' Matthew replied curtly, then thought better of it. 'On the other hand, given your experience of criminal plots, you might be able to assist me there.'

'Later, perhaps. We've both got enough on our plates right now, and my first job has to be to sort my men out, before some of them drift back home to their warm beds. Excuse me.'

Matthew walked briskly back out into Oak Lane, glad to get the circulation back in his toes, and could just make out the general shape of the Carlyle coach as it sat silently in front of a row of tenement houses. As he approached, Collins appeared. 'Where are the Master and Miss Adelaide?'

'They won't be returning immediately,' Matthew told him, 'and in fact they may be absent for a day or two. But I'm working as their assistant in their absence, so would you be prepared to take instructions from me during that time?'

'I wouldn't be doing anything else, would I, and if you say that the Master's approved it, then just say the word. Hopefully we're leaving this dreadful place, so where to next?'

'St Dunstan's,' Matthew instructed him, and climbed into the empty coach.

12

'I take it you have a handkerchief?' Carlyle asked as he and Adelaide stepped back inside the warehouse.

'Of course,' she replied.

'Then hold it firmly over your mouth and nose, as I shall do with mine,' Carlyle instructed. 'For one thing it'll smother the appalling smell, and for another it will act as a filter against accidental infection. In due course, when it gets light and we can find some string, we'll tie them around our heads, so that we can use both hands. I see that you're wearing gloves, but don't take them off, even when — and if — you begin to warm up in here.'

They looked fearfully into the cavernous room with their torches held high in the air. Several of the wretches lying on the floor turned feebly when they saw the flickering light, and one of them waved a wobbly hand in acknowledgment. The smell was almost overpowering, and Adelaide required no instruction to step carefully around each vaguely visible pool of vomit and runny excrement that they were required to sidestep as they weaved their way cautiously through the dozen or so young people lying shivering under what threadbare covering they had managed to acquire and retain.

'Dear God, they're lying on the bare floor,' Carlyle muttered. 'Make a note to ask Jennings for beds as a priority.'

'*Another* priority?' Adelaide queried. 'Where can we even begin to make a start in here?'

'Once it gets light, we'll attend to each one in turn and assess how far gone they are,' her father told her, 'then we'll need to sort them into groups. You'll have to harden yourself to the prospect of abandoning those who're too far gone, so that we can devote more time to the ones we can save.'

Adelaide was just absorbing this unwanted instruction when there was movement above floor level from somewhere near the back of the cavernous room, and a pale face loomed into the light of their torches as they approached.

'Have you brought us food?' came the voice of a boy of around thirteen years of age. 'I'm starving!'

'You feel hungry?' Carlyle asked hopefully. 'Have you managed to avoid all this sickness?'

'No, I was one of the first,' the young boy replied. 'But now I'm feeling better, and I could eat a horse.'

'We didn't bring a horse, I'm afraid,' Carlyle chuckled, 'but what you tell me fills me with considerable hope for the others.'

'Two of them's dead already,' the boy replied. 'They're up near the back there. Bertie Jackson and Jenny Savage.'

'What's your name?' Adelaide asked, and gave a cry of recognition when the boy replied, 'Billy Vane.'

'Your mother thinks you're dead!' Adelaide blurted without thinking, and she saw Billy nodding in the pale circle of light.

'I nearly was, like I said, but now I'm just so hungry and thirsty!'

'Whatever you do, don't eat or drink anything you find in here!' Carlyle told him, his voice tense with urgency. 'We believe you were all poisoned by the water you took from the canal out there, and any food left in here's likely to be contaminated. We've got food and fresh water arriving tomorrow.'

'You mean I can't go home tonight?' Billy demanded.

Carlyle shook his head. 'You may still be carrying the disease, and we can't afford to let you spread it when you go home. Do I gather that you're from St Dunstan's?'

'We all are,' he was told. 'At least, all but Jenny, and she's dead, like I said. She was a school friend of Clarrie Hopgood's, but Clarrie went missing a while ago, and we assumed she'd escaped. Was it Clarrie who told you where to find the rest of us?'

Adelaide fought back the tears, but rather than tell Billy that Clarrie had been fished out of the canal with sickening injuries to her legs, she followed up on something he'd just said. 'What did you mean by "escape", just now? What did she need to escape from?'

'The Man,' Billy replied. 'He's gone now, but everyone's too sick to get out of here. I'd just decided to head for home myself once it got light tomorrow, to get help for the others, but now you tell me I can't.'

'They're all safe now,' Carlyle assured him, 'and it's just a matter of getting them well enough to go home. But this man you just mentioned — what was his name?'

'No idea,' Billy replied. 'We just called him "the Man". He spoke funny — kind of like foreign, you know? He knew enough English to teach us circus tricks, and he told us that we'd be earning lots of money when we put on shows and stuff. But until then we had to steal stuff from other people's houses, and if we refused he got nasty and started punching and kicking us.'

'You were planning on breaking into your parents' house, weren't you?' Adelaide probed. 'Only your mother saw you through the window, and you ran off.'

'Yeah,' Billy confirmed ruefully. 'The Man kicked the shit out of me when we came back with nothing. Oh, sorry, Miss. Aren't you the curate's lady friend?'

'His wife, now,' Adelaide confirmed. 'But this man kicked you, you said?'

'Yeah — I've still got the bruises on my legs. But that's what he did to all of us when we didn't do what he told us, and he said he'd kill us if we tried to escape and he caught us. That's why none of us were brave enough to try it. Except Edgar.'

'Edgar Holroyd?' Adelaide asked eagerly.

Billy nodded. 'Is he safe? Only he had the flu or something, and the Man put him in a room near the back, so that he couldn't give it to the rest of us. The Man was really angry when he found that he'd got away.'

'He's safe, don't worry,' Adelaide reassured him. 'My husband and I found him in the churchyard and nursed him back to health.'

'Can you nurse the rest of those in here?' Billy asked. 'And where's your husband?'

'He's waiting outside,' Adelaide replied, 'but this man's my father, and he's a doctor. If anyone can make the rest of your friends better, he can.'

'That's good,' Billy replied, 'but I'm still hungry.'

'You'll get food in the morning,' Carlyle assured him. 'But until then, can you tell us who the rest of your friends in here are?'

Billy began rattling off a list of names, until Carlyle raised a hand to silence him. 'We can't be expected to remember a list that long,' he chuckled, 'so do you know if there's any paper in here?'

'In a room at the back there,' Billy told him. 'I think it must have been an office or something, because there's lots of paper and pencils in there, and we used to use them for drawing and suchlike when it was raining outside and we couldn't practise our circus tricks.'

'I'll go,' Carlyle offered, and Adelaide watched as the circle of light from his torch wavered uncertainly out of the large room down what looked like some sort of corridor, then disappeared to the right, leaving a faint glow out in the corridor. Adelaide was just wondering how to keep up the conversation with Billy when he supplied her with the opportunity.

'Why are you holding that cloth over your face, Miss? Do I smell that bad, and have you brought me any clean clothes?'

'No, it's not that,' Adelaide told him with a reassuring smile that was probably hidden anyway by the handkerchief over her nose and mouth. 'It's just that the doctor thinks that the young people in here might be infectious. Do you know what that word means?'

'Not really,' Billy admitted, 'but it doesn't sound very nice.'

'I'm afraid it's not. It means that each of you can pass the sickness to each other. By covering up my mouth and nose I can make sure that none of your friends infects me while I'm looking after them. The doctor's covered his face as well, as you saw. You wouldn't want us to get sick, so that we couldn't make the rest of you better again, would you?'

'There was indeed some sort of office back there,' Carlyle told them as he returned with his hands full. He handed Adelaide a length of twine. 'I think they must have used this stuff to tie labels onto their products, but at least we can now tie these makeshift masks around our heads, so let's do that right away.'

'I was just explaining the purpose of those masks to Billy,' Adelaide explained, 'but you seem to have got some paper as well.'

'Indeed I have, along with pencils,' Carlyle confirmed. 'It must have been a very well equipped office, and they must have left in a considerable hurry without making much effort to clear it. I found these little metal stands on which they presumably mounted their price labels, and we can put them to a better use than mere commerce.'

'In what way?' Adelaide asked, but her father's only reply was to instruct her to take the torch from his hand so that he could tie the handkerchief across his mouth and nose. Then he took both torches in order to allow Adelaide to do the same with hers. Once she'd done that, he handed her back the second torch as he muttered, 'Life will become so much easier when daylight returns,' before experimenting with one of the former price stands and a blank price label. 'Excellent!' he remarked, as he looked back up at Billy and Adelaide.

'Very well, young man,' he said to Billy. 'Time for you to introduce us to your friends. My daughter here will write their names on one of these pieces of paper, which we'll insert into a stand and leave alongside where they're lying. That way, we won't need to keep asking them their names.'

Very slowly, with Billy in charge of Adelaide's torch so as to free up her hands, they worked their way through the uneven ranks of those who lay in their own filth, groaning, begging for water, or simply staring blankly back up at them.

'Timmy Broadbent,' Billy told them as they stopped at the first of them.

While Adelaide was busy writing the name on the tag and placing it in the frame, her father reached out a gloved hand to test the pulse below his jaw line, then raise his top eyelid to stare down into his eyes. 'Write the number "1" below his name,' he instructed her, and she did as requested.

Next in the line was a boy who didn't even open his eyes as they settled next to him, and Adelaide duly wrote 'Peter Dutton' and '3', as instructed. And so on through the ragged line of children lying on the bare wooden floor, wet with indescribable fluids, until they had accounted for all but the two dead ones.

'Why did you get me to allocate them all numbers?' Adelaide asked as they sat near the entrance door, having instructed Billy to go through to one of the rooms at the back, to keep well away from the others, and to try to get some sleep.

'Ever heard of something called "triage"?' Carlyle asked, and when she shook her head he went into lecture mode. 'The word is French, and translates literally as "sort". French doctors have begun to employ it at the scenes of disasters such as train wrecks, or building collapses, and I learned it from a French surgeon who was visiting the London Hospital, researching into the Elephant Man. Put simply, you separate a large number of patients into categories when you don't have enough resources to treat them all at once. The categories indicate the degree of urgency, the most urgent receiving first call on the available facilities, the next most urgent the second level, and so on.'

'So what does "three" mean, of those numbers that we allocated just now?'

Carlyle hesitated, but realised that he had no choice but to explain. 'Try not to get upset, but those I designated as a three we can do nothing for. They give the impression that their bodies have already begun the internal close-down indicative of impending death. Low pulse rate, lack of blood coursing through veins, probably liver and kidney failure, and irregular breathing. All we can do for them is pain relief, if they're still conscious enough to be experiencing any.'

'So we do what — just leave them to die?' Adelaide asked judgmentally.

Her father nodded. 'The reality of imperfect medicine, I'm afraid. Console yourself with the rewarding experience of saving those who *can* be saved.'

'And they're numbers one and two?' she asked hopefully.

He nodded. 'The "ones" have already begun to recover, which is why they're surrounded by so much of their own corruption. Their bodies have rejected so much of the contagion that it's given up and gone looking for another place to breed. In one sense they're the most dangerous to others around them — and don't for one moment lose sight of the fact that this includes us — but they're destined to survive. We must concentrate on the number "two" category, of which, from memory, we have four. By keeping up their body fluids we give the contagion something to fasten onto while it works through their systems.'

Adelaide fell silent, and eventually a tear slid down one cheek. Her father took her gloved hand in his, and smiled encouragingly. 'Do you now perhaps understand why I never seemed to encourage you to follow me into medicine? You care too much — that makes you a superb nurse, but a rather unreliable doctor. Now let's try to sleep for an hour or two.'

'You're not serious, I take it?' Chief Inspector Bradbury demanded as John Jennings stood before his office desk looking decidedly uncomfortable. He'd just done his best to explain why he needed six men on rotational twelve-hour shifts in Limehouse, and was armed with a list of items for purchase or other acquisition that seemed adequate to put an entire army into the field.

'It's not of my choosing, sir,' Jennings wheedled. 'It's Doctor Carlyle who insisted on all this, and if it were left to me, the little Arabs could be left to die in there, given that they must have effected an unlawful entry in the first place. Although I'm told that the man behind it all is someone wanted for murder, and we should be better able to buckle him if the children can be persuaded to peach on his whereabouts.'

'Even so, the cost in manpower and money!' Bradbury reminded him, and Jennings opted to hang his head in silence, since he could think of nothing more to add. 'Tell me again why we can't just toss the place and bring the little shits out of there in restraints?'

The reference to "shits" reminded Jennings that he still had the worst news to impart, and he now had little option, if he was to be granted the resources needed in Limehouse.

'Cholera, sir.'

'Beg pardon?'

'According to the good doctor, they're suffering from cholera, so we need to keep them isolated.'

'Why didn't you say that in the first place?' Bradbury demanded. 'Are you telling me that if we go in there, or allow the place to be flushed out, these urchins are likely to bring about another cholera epidemic?'

'That's what the doctor said, sir,' Jennings confirmed, sensing a change of mood and a light at the end of a very murky tunnel.

'Well, we can't have that, can we?' Bradbury asked rhetorically. 'You can have what you're asking for, but keep a tight note of every shilling we commit, and be prepared to account for every one of them in due course. And don't come back in here with cholera yourself.'

Matthew instructed Collins to drive the coach into the warehouse yard and turn it, ready for departure. He climbed down, and with the coachman's assistance lifted a heavy box from the roof rack and laid it on the ground.

St Mary-le-Bow was booming out ten in the forenoon, and Matthew had been shopping. In the box were a dozen pairs of ladies' and gents' gloves, a matching number of handkerchiefs, and two weighty-looking tomes from the bookshop, both of which had 'Florence Nightingale' on their title pages. Neither of them were books *about* the lady; instead, they were written by the lady herself, with the grand titles of *Notes on Nursing: What It Is and What It Is Not* and *Cassandra.* He sat on the mounting board with the coach door swinging open in the chill wind, and began flicking through the second of these, then opened his eyes in disbelief. No wonder Carlyle had wanted Adelaide to read these while imprisoned behind the doors of the warehouse cum makeshift hospital — it was as if Adelaide herself had written the book, with entire paragraphs about the undervaluing of women in contemporary society, the useless idleness to which they were condemned as wives and mothers, and a good deal else regarding male attitudes towards women in general.

He looked up sharply as he sensed movement in the doorway across the yard, but his hopes sank when he saw that it was Carlyle himself, removing some sort of mask from his face, taking a few deep breaths, then reaching into his jacket pocket for a cigar. Matthew lifted the box and carried it towards his father-in-law, calling out on his way across. Carlyle smiled as he blew cigar smoke into the stiff breeze, and his breath formed a cloud as he called back in response.

'If you were hoping to see Adelaide, then I'm sorry to disappoint you,' he said. 'Before you enquire, she's in perfect health, if a little stunned by what confronted us in there. I've let her sleep in — if you could call curling under one's own overcoat on a hard wooden floor "sleeping in" — since she has an even more challenging day ahead of her. When Jennings turns up, tell him to lose no time in having the first two graves dug, and then no doubt you'll need to pray over them or something. More to the immediate point, tell Jennings that I need a dozen of those pallet things that they install in prison cells for their victims to lie on. The poor buggers in there are lying on the floor in their own filth.'

Matthew grimaced. Then he put down the box in order to display its contents. 'Handkerchiefs and gloves for you both, as requested. I wasn't sure if you had an account with Bainbridges in Whitechapel Road, but you do now, because I just opened one with a substantial debit balance. I told them I was your personal priest, and by some miracle they believed me. Also these two books for Adelaide.'

Carlyle looked at the two titles and smiled. 'Excellent. I think that Adelaide will appreciate *Cassandra* in particular.'

'You know of it?'

'Indeed, I possess a copy,' Carlyle said. 'It was one of my late wife's favourites.'

'Then why…?'

'Why did I send you to acquire another one? So as not to reveal to Adelaide that I already had a copy which I'd kept hidden from her for years. It was locked in my office cabinet in the years during which my daughter was learning to fly without the assistance of her late mother's wings. She seemed to possess enough revolutionary fervour without my adding to it. But I think that the time has come.' A wagon rumbled into the yard, and half a dozen men jumped from its open back and sides, wielding shovels and picks. 'Here come your gravediggers, at a guess, so I'll leave it to you to tell them where to plant their implements.'

'Two dead, you said?' Matthew asked. 'Do you remember their names, by any chance?'

'I have them written here, on this piece of paper, which I won't hand to you, in case I pass some sort of contagion onto you, even through a gloved hand and a sterile piece of paper. You're about to receive the corpses of Herbert Jackson and Jenny Savage. Ring any bells?'

Matthew nodded. 'Bertie Jackson was one of mine. An only child, and his father's a sick man. They'll take the news hard.'

'But not yet, as we agreed,' Carlyle reminded him. 'And they won't be the last, I'm afraid.'

13

Matthew suddenly had nothing to do, aside from supervising the digging up of the cobbles in the yard in order to create a crude burial ground. He certainly had no parish duties, thanks to the scheming Holroyds, and all that was immediately important to him was down here in a disused furniture warehouse in Limehouse, so he might as well hang around and see what transpired.

He wandered over to the wagon that had recently delivered the workmen with their picks and shovels. The wagon was covered by canvas signs on which were displayed the name "Commercial Gas Light and Coke Company", and it came to a halt only a few yards short of the main doors to the former warehouse. A tall man descended from the running board and walked up to Matthew with a business-like air, then looked down in disappointment at his dog collar.

'Well, you ain't the police, anyroad, so where is 'e?'

'Where's who?' Matthew asked.

The man checked the work sheet in his hand. 'Inspector Jennings, it sez 'ere. We was told ter reconnect the gas in that there warehouse, but I'll need 'is signature.'

'Won't mine do?' Matthew asked hopefully, but the man shook his head.

'It 'as ter be the bloke what instructed it, see? Them's regulations, an' yer can't muck around wi' gas. I suppose I can go inside an' find the input.'

'You can't go in there,' Matthew insisted in alarm. 'It's not safe.' He broke into a smile as what looked like a travelling circus turned into the yard from the street outside. There were at least four wagons, and on the front board of the leading wagon sat a man whose pork pie hat was familiar enough even from that distance. 'Here's the man you're looking for,' Matthew told the gas man as he hurried across the yard to meet the leading coach.

'The gas company's here ahead of you, to reconnect the mains,' he told Jennings as he looked up at where he was seated, 'but their foreman, or whoever he is, reckons that they need to go inside to do the job.'

Jennings sighed and climbed down from the wagon. 'I can see it's going to be one of those days. Is that the bloke over there?'

Matthew confirmed that Jennings had identified the right person, and Jennings was soon waving his arms in animated conversation. Finally he walked back to Matthew, shaking his head. 'You'll have to let him in there if you want the gas reconnected,' he insisted, 'so I'll leave that bit to you, while I get these wagons unloaded.'

Matthew had no option but to hammer on the wooden front doors with the side of his fist. Then he stood back, hoping that it would be Adelaide who answered his summons; however, it was Carlyle, his face covered almost entirely by a large pocket handkerchief tied around his head with some heavy industrial twine.

'What is it?' he asked grumpily. 'We're just about to start organising for the first of the bodies to come out — have you got the graves dug yet?'

'Graves?' the gas foreman echoed weakly.

Carlyle nodded towards him. 'Who's he?' he demanded, and Matthew explained.

'He's from the gas company, and he insists that he has to come inside in order to reconnect your supply.'

'Out of the question,' Carlyle snapped. 'It's too risky.'

'Look, mate,' the peeved gas man responded. 'I don't know what Devil's work yer up to in there, but if yer wants gas, yer got ter let me in, see? Only I'm not ser sure I wants ter come in anyroad, since it all looks kind've creepy in there, an' it don't smell too good, neither.'

'Where exactly inside *is* the gas connection?' Carlyle demanded. 'In my house it's just inside the front door.'

'I can see it from 'ere,' the man replied, 'an' that's just about as far as I wants ter come inter this creepy place. It's that box thing just behind yer.'

'Wait there,' Carlyle instructed him as he closed the doors in both their faces, emerging shortly afterwards holding a large pocket handkerchief and two lengths of twine. 'Tie that across your face,' he ordered the gas man.

'Bloody rare carry on this is, an' no mistake,' the man muttered as he did as instructed. Then he made short work of turning a valve on the input box with a specially tooled spanner that he removed from his working overalls, after which he scuttled back outside and threw the makeshift mask onto the ground.

Carlyle closed the doors firmly once more, and Matthew was left staring at the gas man, who was considerably paler in the face than he had been earlier.

'I've done some funny places in me time,' he muttered. 'Workhouses, 'ospitals, prisons, an' even the odd mad'ouse, but I ain't never encountered owt like what yer've got in there. An' you a parson an' all. What's the go in there, matey? Yer caught a few demons from 'ell, or what?'

'None of your business,' Matthew replied bluntly. 'Thank you for your attendance, and now I imagine that you have other jobs to attend, so I won't keep you.'

'Wild 'orses wouldn't keep me 'ere, me friend. So I bid yer a good day, an' I'll be gone as soon as I've got a signature from that other weird cove over there.'

He strode purposefully over to where Jennings was directing the unloading of a consignment of pallets used in police station cells to allow more favoured prisoners to lie down at night. Next to those was a collection of hampers, one of which had an open lid that revealed its contents to be at least a dozen loaves.

'Careful with those vinegar jars,' Jennings called to a cart driver near the rear of the line, then he turned to the two men on the water carrier and instructed them to start filling the enormous water jugs that had just been lifted off the first wagon.

'Bloody weird, an' no mistake,' the gas man muttered to himself as he got the all-important signature and lost no time in urging his horse out of the yard, still shaking his head.

'It looks as if the things we need are being unloaded at the doors,' Carlyle told Adelaide as she came back from lighting all the gas jets in the walls, and the gas fires with which every room seemed to be equipped. 'What order do you think we should do things in?' he added. 'After all, you're the one with the more recent ward experience — I just go between the beds on my routine rounds.'

'I've been giving that some thought,' Adelaide replied. 'Since you've divided up the patients into three groups, I suggest that we convert two of the rooms down the corridor into wards. And now that we can see what we're doing, we'd better move the bodies somewhere out of sight until we can bury them. Since the category two patients are going to need most of our attention, I suggest that we leave them here in this larger room, with the category ones in the first empty room back there, and the threes further back.'

Carlyle gazed at her admiringly. 'You're clearly a born nurse,' he said, 'and it shall be as you wish. Once we've got the beds in here, we'll need to lift the more seriously afflicted onto them, so let's start by getting the beds in. Then we have the highly unpleasant task of cleaning up the floors where they've been lying, for which we'll need the mops and cloths. Finally you'll need to mix vinegar with water, in what I suggest should be a strong proportion, and swill everything clean.'

'When can we begin to give them water?' Adelaide asked solicitously. 'They keep crying out for it, and we need to keep up their body fluids, or so you told me. I can't bear to listen to their tortured pleas for much longer.'

'Nothing to eat or drink until we've sanitised the place properly, I'm afraid,' her father told her. 'So the sooner we get that finished, the better. Time to open up briefly and get in the supplies, so try to keep your eyes off Matthew. He was out there the last time I was, and this is no time for lovers' reunions.'

The day wore on, with frustrations for both Matthew and Adelaide. Carlyle insisted on being the one who periodically ventured outside to collect the supplies they needed, fearful that somehow his daughter and her husband would find it impossible not to embrace, or even kiss, for a brief moment, thereby taking the infection out into the wider community. Every time that the double doors slid open cautiously a few inches Matthew prayed that Adelaide's slim form would appear in the gap, but every time his heart leapt at the prospect, it was as if someone had doused it with cold water when all that appeared was the gaunt figure of her father, his face hidden by a white kerchief.

By the middle of the day the first two graves had been dug, and two mounds of muddy soil had replaced the neatly laid cobbles alongside the wall, where two holes a few feet in depth had been dug in the loamy ground. More cobbles to the side had been raised in anticipation of two more graves being dug, but for the time being the labourers were huddled around their cart, eating the dinners they'd brought with them, and swilling down cold tea from sealed jars.

Matthew was building up his hopes that Adelaide would sooner or later be required to emerge from her self-imposed exile among the dead and the dying, if only to assist her father to drag out the two bodies that he'd been told to expect, and for that reason he declined Jennings's invitation to join him in a nearby pub for a meat pie. 'Please yourself,' the bored officer replied, 'but why hang around here?'

'Adelaide and her father will need to bring the bodies out eventually, and I don't want to miss it when they do,' Matthew replied. 'Don't take all your men with you, in case I need a hand to deepen the graves and throw the bodies in.'

'I'm not taking *any* of them with me,' Jennings replied with an upturned nose, 'since discipline is discipline, and it'll be bad enough that one of us is drinking on duty.'

'Where are your men, anyway?' Matthew asked. 'If you instructed them to remain inconspicuous, they certainly obeyed that order. The ones who'd been on nightshift were huddled against that left hand wall when I first got here this morning, but this latest lot seem to have gone missing in action.'

'They're skilled in surreptitious surveillance,' Jennings replied, 'but now that they've decided to light a bonfire to keep out the winter chill, they're about as invisible as that new Tower Bridge.' He nodded towards the front face of another building to the right of the main warehouse, where a thin plume of smoke was rising. 'I'll bring you back a chicken pie if you like,' he added cheerily as he turned and made his way out of the yard.

A thought struck Matthew, and he walked over to where a half a dozen police officers in their ordinary street clothes were warming their hands over a rudimentary bonfire, to the side of which were several long pieces of what looked like abandoned packing cases. 'Where did the wood come from?' Matthew asked.

One of them nodded towards the building behind them. 'In there. Looks like some sort of storage place, although they made it bloody tall for a wood store.'

'Did you leave any wood in there?'

'Yeah, there's heaps left,' he was told, and he wandered across, prised open the door that was already ajar and peered inside. There was a scuttling noise like a family of rats making themselves scarce, and he picked his way carefully through the abandoned refuse until he found what he was looking for. He carried four pieces of pallet wood and a few sections of cut twine out into the open, then made his way to where the two open graves awaited their residents. He searched among the discarded loam in a pile to one side until he found a sharply pointed stone, then chose the darkest piece of wood he'd been able to find, and laboriously carved the name of Herbert Jackson into it. He couldn't quite remember the name of the other dead child, since she was, he recalled, a girl from another parish, but he'd have time enough to carve her headstone later. He then lashed the horizontal piece at right angles to a longer vertical piece, then drove the completed crude cross into the soil mound at the side. It was rudimentary, but it was the best he could do.

As he stood up and straightened his back muscles, Matthew became aware of a group of people standing just inside the entrance to the warehouse yard, and in the continuing absence of Inspector Jennings he decided to enquire regarding their business. As he approached them, he did his best to guess who they might be; they clearly had no work to go to, and they were shabbily dressed, so his guess was that they were the idle and curious from neighbouring streets.

'Can I help you in some way?' he asked politely, and the shortest of the three, who turned out to be a woman in her mid to late thirties, dressed with all the elegance of a coal heaver, pierced him with the sort of stare that demanded the truth, and which no doubt terrified instant confessions out of any children she might have.

'Yer searchin' fer them ghosts in there?' she demanded.

'What ghosts?' Matthew asked disingenuously, but a rat-faced man by her side snorted in derision.

'Don't try an' snow us, mate. We bin 'earing' the ghosts o' them young 'uns fer days nah. We only lives round the corner from 'ere, an' we 'ears 'em callin' fer their mummies every night.' He seemed to become aware of Matthew's dog collar, and pointed at it as he told the others, 'See that? They brung in a priest ter exorcise the bleedin' dead!'

'I'm only a regular Church of England curate,' Matthew insisted.

'So why yer exorcisin' ghosts?' came the illogical reply from another man on the fringe of the small group.

Matthew shook his head. 'I'm not, really I'm not.'

'Well, yer not from round 'ere,' the first woman objected. 'So where yer from?'

'St Dunstan's, in Stepney,' Matthew told them, instantly regretting having done so. 'And there's really nothing to see here, so I suggest that you move on.'

'There were a gas bloke in the pub around dinner time,' the rat-faced man persisted, 'an' 'e were tellin' anyone what'd listen that there's a bloke inside that there old furniture place what 'ad 'is face covered wi' a white mask, an' were talkin' about bringin' bodies outta there. So if there's nowt goin' on in there, 'ow come there's bodies? Tell us that, then.'

'Move along there!' came a stern voice from halfway up the street as Inspector Jennings came into sight, waving his police badge high in the air. 'This is no place for you lot to be hanging around. So move on before I do you for obstruction.'

The group wandered away down the street, muttering to themselves, but the ferret-faced man couldn't resist one more verbal shot as he stopped and yelled back, 'There *must* be sumfin goin' on in there, if they needs Peelers ter guard the place.'

Jennings and Matthew exchanged concerned looks as they turned and walked back into the yard.

'Do you think we're going to attract a crowd?' Matthew asked.

Jennings nodded. 'Especially when we start bringing bodies out,' he confirmed.

It was starting to get dark early, given the time of year, by the time that the warehouse doors opened yet again, for long enough to allow Carlyle and Adelaide to roll a couple of inert bundles out onto the cobbles. Adelaide hung back, and Matthew hurried over towards her. She slid back inside until only her head was still visible, and Matthew called out.

'Don't disappear completely, darling! I've been waiting all day for a chance to see you!'

'Just be grateful you're not close enough to smell me,' she grimaced back. 'That's why I hoped you'd still be here. When you go home, can you bring me back some fresh undergarments? You know where I keep them, don't you?'

'Yes, under your skirt and blouse,' he joked, but she showed no sign of amusement.

'I'm serious — I've been wearing these for two days. Don't let me down! And don't open those bundles — just bury them as they are, and we'll arrange for the lime to be poured on once you've gone. All of you.' With that she slipped back inside, leaving Matthew feeling cheated.

Jennings called three of his men over to assist, and they carried the bundles carefully over to the two open graves. The gravediggers had departed, but at Matthew's request they'd left a shovel, and it was the work of only a few minutes to cover over the pathetic remains wrapped tightly in what looked like old ships' canvas tied tightly at head and foot. One of the bundles had been considerably lighter than the other, which Matthew assumed was the corpse of Herbert Jackson. He opted to bury him first. He therefore hammered the crude cross more firmly into the ground at the head of the makeshift grave with the aid of the shovel, and then said a prayer for the soul of the poor boy taken before his time.

As he raised his eyes from the grave he saw three figures peering furtively over the low wall near the entrance gate, and sighed heavily as he turned to Jennings.

'Don't look now, but we're being watched. I dread to think what stories will be doing the rounds by tomorrow morning.'

Adelaide was exhausted, hungry, thirsty, anxious, and — by her standards — very smelly. It was her second night in this dreadful place that felt like a prison, surrounded by the sick and the dying, spending her days mopping up stinking piles of other people's bodily fluids, and washing floors with diluted vinegar. But this was surely the essence of nursing? People didn't need nurses when they were well — only when they were sick and vulnerable. For the dozen or so wretched souls in here — all of them doubly vulnerable because they were children — she was the only source of succour in their hour of direst need, and the only hope that they would survive. She owed a great obligation both to them and to their parents.

Even so, most nurses had the opportunity to bathe, eat, drink and live in a modicum of comfort once their hours of duty on the wards were completed, but she seemed to be denied even that. She and her father had decided to claim two rooms for themselves towards the rear of the building, down the long corridor that was gloomy even in the middle of the day because there were no gas lights fitted in it. They'd each claimed a pallet to lie on when exhaustion overcame them, but the former warehouse appeared to have possessed no washing facilities — and why should it have done? — and only one lavatory that was of the 'earth closet' type, with a bucket that required emptying after heavy use. Since she and her father were the only two ambulant people in the building, and since neither of them was eating or drinking much, for fear of ingesting infection, the need to empty the bucket was not a pressing one, but it had been added to her other duties.

As for her patients, there had been little change in the two days during which she had walked routinely between them with a mug of water here, a reassuring smile there, and always the mop and the rags to remove their embarrassment at their own incontinence. There was one more body to bury, and two of the category two patients were hanging in a parlous balance between life and death, but it was encouraging to hear the category ones calling for water and attempting to rise to their feet.

She lay back wearily on her pallet, thinking of Matthew and their comfortable home. She replayed in her mind the few occasions upon which she'd been allowed a brief sight of him that day, and this triggered another more recent memory. Curious as well as bored, she reached across to the old packing case that she was using as a crude form of bedside table, and took one of the books he'd left her that morning. It was one of those by Florence Nightingale, of whom she'd heard, but about whom she knew next to nothing. It was called *Cassandra*, and she opened the shiny half-calf cover, lay back, and began to read.

By the time that sleep overtook her, the book falling down on her chest, she'd entered another world. A world that she had always hoped existed, but which she had never seen described in print.

14

Matthew tutted with irritation when he heard the knock on the door. He was only just home, and was hoping to cook himself something tasty for supper before sliding into a cold solitary bed, but before he could forget Adelaide's last request, he'd opened her 'unmentionables' drawer and extracted all the lacy, silken undergarments he could find in there. He'd been in the hallway, where they kept their travelling bags, searching for a suitable receptacle in which to convey them down to Limehouse the following morning, when the knock came on the front door a few feet away. His arms still full of ladies' undergarments, he reached out and opened it. There stood Joseph Mulholland.

The vicar looked down with raised eyebrows at what Matthew was clutching to his chest, and Matthew burst out laughing.

'Don't worry,' he assured Mulholland, 'I'm not indulging in some dubious hobby. These are for Adelaide, who's working away with her father for a few days.'

'Yes, Beatrice and I had noticed that you'd both been missing for a day or two. Are you working with them?'

'In one sense, yes, hence the need to take more clothing for Adelaide. But it's not as if I'm required for parish duties, is it?' he added sourly.

Mulholland nodded. 'No, obviously not, and I really am deeply sorry for the situation in which you find yourself. Believe me when I say that I'm making every effort to get to the bottom of the mystery, and that I'll advise you as soon as I do. One way or the other, of course.'

'Yes, quite,' Matthew replied sadly. 'I thought that's why you might be calling at this late hour — to tell me that my name had been cleared.'

'It's late in the evening because we noticed the lights from your windows, and we hadn't seen you around the place during the day. I have a message for you. A man called Timothy something or other came looking for you. He'd been told that you were based here, seemingly by someone in Limehouse, and he wanted to speak with you. He said that he was a friend of your sister, and that he works as a newspaper reporter.'

Matthew groaned. Timothy Washbourne was the last person on earth he wished to talk with, at this time or any other. An ambitious but treacherous newspaper journalist who published his stories with a view to promoting his own career rather than informing his readers of the truth, Tim Washbourne had for a while paid court to Matthew's younger sister Caroline, both with a view to seducing her and with half an eye to getting the 'inside story' on Matthew's first encounter with Carlyle and his daughter, when an unscrupulous alleged psychic medium had announced that 'devils from Hell' had been unleashed via the bowels of the underground network at Aldgate Station. During the ensuing public panic, Matthew had been confronted by the man who was behind it all, and had fought with him in the street, allowing Timothy Washbourne to publish several columns of rubbish about the brave clergyman who'd taken on the Devil Incarnate and won.

No, Timothy Washbourne was not someone whose acquaintance Matthew wished to renew, and following Mulholland's departure his heart sank as he sat at the kitchen table, head in hands, and cursed himself for allowing Washbourne to learn of his activities in Limehouse. Matthew had unwittingly revealed both his identity and his current position to some old crone in the street who'd accused him of being some sort of exorcist, and she'd no doubt earned herself a few more glasses of stout or gin by contacting the *Telegraph* and offering them a story about spooky goings on alongside the already infamous Limehouse Cut. As if he didn't have enough to worry about.

Adelaide was awoken from a restless slumber by her father shaking her gently by the shoulder. 'We have work to do that we can only do in darkness,' he told her as she rose groggily to her feet and suppressed the oath that came most readily to her mind.

'The new body?' she asked.

He nodded. 'Plus the two that we've already had buried, which also need to be limed. Follow me.'

Having wrapped the body of Nicholas Wainwright tightly in one of the lengths of canvas that had presumably been used by the former occupants of the building to wrap goods intended for horse-drawn travel Carlyle and Adelaide grunted their way to the front doors and rolled the deceased onto the cobbles. There was a sudden movement to their right, where some sort of bonfire was burning down to its embers, and a burly man came into sight.

'Keep your distance, unless you want cholera!' Carlyle urged him, and the constable required no further warning as he stepped backwards several paces.

'Keep your eyes peeled while we bury this one,' was the next instruction, and a few moments later Nicholas Wainright had reached his final resting place four feet down, alongside the other two graves. Carlyle cursed softly, then gave Adelaide further instructions. 'We need to go back inside for the lime, and two buckets of water. The first two graves have already been covered, but if we pour the lime on top, then add water, it'll form a protective crust of sorts, and we can give instruction for more earth to be raked over it in daylight. This latest one can be limed directly.'

It took them fifteen minutes to complete this operation, and Adelaide looked up as she heard the distant sound of voices, then squinted through the freezing fog towards the entrance gate. 'There seem to be people out there watching us,' she told her father, who chuckled.

'It's probably the most exciting thing this miserable dump of a place has seen since they originally dug that canal, and the first barges headed out towards the Thames. Anyway, come on — I'm beginning to shiver from the cold.'

Back inside, they were wafting their arms across their chests in order to warm themselves when a thin figure loomed out of the flickering gaslight in the main room and began walking towards them with an unsteady gait.

'Can I have something to eat, please?' the girl asked, and Carlyle gave a cry of triumph.

'Our first success! God be praised!'

Adelaide almost burst into tears as she replied to the request. 'Certainly, Emily. Go and lie back down and I'll bring you some bread and dripping. And thank you for giving me the inspiration to keep going!'

Matthew cursed under his breath as he heard the whining voice a few feet behind him, wishing him a good morning. If there was anything good about it, it was because he was closer to Adelaide, back here in the yard. So near, yet so far. He turned with a snarl that was uncharacteristic of him, but well deserved in Timothy Washbourne's case.

'Go away, or I'll tell my sister that you're suffering from the pox.'

'Tell her what you like, since I'm now engaged to be married to the daughter of my News Editor. But I'm not the only one who's come up in the world, am I? So what brings you to this benighted spot? Still pursuing demons?'

'I never was, and if you don't leave now, there are several police officers over there who'll throw you out on your miserable little arse!'

'Such language from a Man of God!' Washbourne taunted him. 'Now I *know* you're mixed up in something spooky, else you'd have given me the whole story without hesitation. The neighbours have reported your strange antics, and I thought that I owed it to you to allow you to explain it in your own words, but have it your own way. "See you in court", as we muckraking journalists have a habit of saying.'

Matthew watched him leave the yard, if only to satisfy himself that he had, then wandered across to the graves to pray for the souls of their incumbents. He felt guilty that they'd been dumped unceremoniously in holes in the forecourt of a former warehouse, but consoled himself that the decision to do so had not been his. And if they hadn't been buried, then other lives would have been at risk. He noted with added sadness that there was now a third grave, and made a mental note to enquire whose it was.

Hearing a familiar voice from the doorway of the makeshift hospital he looked up, and his spirits rose as he saw Adelaide, peering from the safety of the slightly open doorway and calling to the constables who were seated around their seemingly endless bonfire, and who called back in response to what sounded like a question from her. Matthew grabbed the clothing bag and ran hopefully towards the door, only to experience the humiliation of seeing his own wife of only a few weeks seemingly scrambling inside to avoid him.

'I brought you some clean drawers!' he called out, to the titters of the constables around the bonfire as he laid the bag down at the door.

'Tell the whole of London, why don't you?' Adelaide called back with a chuckle as she peered out again from behind the safety of the doors. 'But thank you, anyway — I was beginning to disgust even myself.'

'Whose is the third body?' Matthew asked.

'Nicholas Wainwright. But there's good news. Emily Freeman's up and walking, demanding food. That's why I was talking to the constables, demanding to know if they'd snaffled the remaining loaves from where we'd left them just inside the door. They say they didn't, but they must have done, so please keep a closer eye on them.'

'That's not my job,' Matthew reminded her. 'But are you saying that food has gone missing?'

'Just two of those long breadstick things, but they were the last, and poor little Emily's needing something to eat. When Jennings comes back, please make sure that he's brought us more food, and if not tell him to go and get some. And we'll need more dripping as well.'

'I fried myself some bacon this morning!' he announced proudly, to which she replied, 'Lucky you. I hope you didn't leave the kitchen in a mess.'

'I love you, Adelaide West.'

'And I love you, Matthew West. Thank you for those books, by the way. Florence Nightingale's a woman after my own heart.'

'Perhaps I should get her to give me my next cooking lesson,' he joked, so happy to be having this lengthy conversation. The mood was, however, short-lived as she extended an arm through the door, picked up the clothing bag, and said, 'Now I have to go back in.'

Matthew gazed sadly at the closed doors, then wandered over to where the duty constables were stacking more wood on the fire. 'Did any of you lot pilfer some bread from inside those doors?' he asked.

The men looked at each other with an amused expression, and one of them answered for them all. 'You *are* joking, I take it? We don't want to catch cholera. Maybe it was the ghost.'

'Don't *you* start,' Matthew groaned. 'The locals are convinced that this place is haunted, mainly due to the children crying out before we got here.'

'Well, two of us definitely heard a man's cough,' another constable replied. 'It was the middle of the night, and as quiet as the grave. It came from over in that building where we get the wood for the fire, so once the sun broke through we went in there in twos, and brought enough out to make sure that we won't need to go in there tomorrow night, unless the day shift use up the lot. Where are the buggers, anyway? It's gone ten o'clock.'

They were no doubt even more delighted than Matthew to see the wagons rolling into the yard a few minutes later. While the shifts were in the process of changing, Matthew walked over to Jennings and enquired if he'd brought any more food. Satisfied that he had, Matthew walked back to the third grave, recited a suitable commitment prayer for the poor boy's soul, then decided that he might as well go home, where at least he could keep warm.

Later that evening, when Matthew awoke from a half slumber by the dying fire in his living room, it was to an imperious knock on the front door. He sighed, got up, and walked down the hall to answer the door, wrenching it open grumpily with the intention of telling Timothy Washbourne where to stick his further enquiries. He pulled up sharply when he saw the gangling outline of the vicar in the gloomy glow cast by the hall lights.

'Good evening,' he said politely. 'It's a little late for a social call, isn't it?'

'It won't be very sociable, I'm afraid,' Mulholland replied angrily as he waved a newspaper under Matthew's nose. 'I just want you to explain this rubbish in the late edition! And it had better be good, or else your suspension will prove to be permanent!'

15

Matthew groaned more than once as he read the pernicious drivel that Timothy Washbourne had written by way of revenge for their brief confrontation that morning. He certainly never let the truth get in the way of a promising 'exclusive', and no doubt his future father-in-law had chuckled gleefully before signing the chitty that sent the story down to the composing room in time for the evening edition of the *Telegraph*. There on the main news page, for all to drool over, he read:

DEMON-SLAYER RETURNS TO THE FRAY
Exclusive report by Timothy Washbourne

Devoted readers of this column will no doubt remember the bravery and death-defying activities of one Matthew West, then a humble Wesleyan preacher attached to the East End Mission in Shadwell. He took on, with his bare hands, the Beast from Hades who had brought up through the London Underground network an army of vengeful spirits of those buried in a Plague pit in Aldgate disturbed by the digging of the subterranean extensions. This dogged reporter can now reveal that the same Matthew West, now the curate of St Dunstan's Church in Stepney, has once again donned his battle armour in order to defy the denizens of the Underworld.

Local residents of Limehouse have long been plagued by ghostly visitations once darkness descends upon this twilight world alongside the Regent's Canal as it enters Limehouse Cut on its way to the Dock Basin. These ghastly emanations have centred on the now abandoned warehouse that was formally tenanted by Peebles, a soft furnishing manufacturer, along the east bank of the Limehouse Cut. It is unclear why these worthy people moved out of their premises so quickly almost a year ago, but could it be that they were driven out by ghostly occurrences? Certainly, since then, those who have the misfortune to live alongside the eerily abandoned building, which shimmers in the moonlight with a ghastly light that can only have a supernatural origin, have reported spine-chilling experiences.

Chief among these has been the wailing of banshee children calling for their Satanic progenitors to bring them human souls to feed on. From time to time a shadow will be seen loping stealthily down its outer walls in the luminous glow of a full moon, while at certain times of day it is possible to see Spirit children at play, no doubt cheered on from inside by the dark forces that command this entire Nursery of Hell.

Undaunted, the Reverend West has assembled a team of resolute and fearless Warriors of Light to battle against the Devil's own, exorcising the pestilence from the very ground, and confining the unholy visitants inside the building, which since the doors were finally sealed on this ghastly playground has been closely guarded by teams of officers from Scotland Yard, specially trained in occult defence. They are visited daily by the saintly Reverend West, who is vigilant around the clock to blast back to the Hell from which they came any Evil Spirits that batter their way through the strong psychic shield that he has woven around the place.

Your dedicated reporter, who is in daily contact with the Reverend West, will continue to report as matters progress.

'You would agree, would you not, that a full and frank explanation is required for this nonsense that appears to quote you as its implied source?' Mulholland demanded.

Matthew nodded. 'That's the least I can do,' he replied meekly, 'but you may find the truth even more unpalatable.'

'At this very moment,' Mulholland muttered through clenched teeth, 'nothing could be more unpalatable to me than to read of my curate being associated with utter hogwash about ghosts, devils, creatures from the Underworld and other assorted "Penny Dreadful" themes.'

'Would you allow me to make us both tea?' Matthew asked in a small voice. 'Not only am I in dire need of one, but it will lubricate my tonsils while I do my best to explain to you something I should have brought to your attention from the very start, but which I shrank from recounting because it was so distressing.'

'To do with your immediate past as a pretended slayer of demons, you mean?' Mulholland demanded accusingly. 'Or are you one of those deluded Spiritualist types?'

'Neither of those accusations is either accurate or fair,' Matthew protested as he put the pan on to boil, and measured the tea into the pot, before apologising for not heating it first.

'Never mind the damned tea!' Mulholland bellowed. 'What is all this about? Do you actually know this Washbourne character, and is he the same "Washbourne" who came enquiring after you the other day?'

'Yes on both counts,' Matthew conceded, 'but he and I are far from being friends, and this entire piece was written in revenge for my not telling him what's *really* going on down in Limehouse.'

'But presumably you're about to tell me?'

'Indeed I am, but one moment while I pour the water into the pot. Is an arrowroot biscuit out of the question?'

'Damn the biscuits — and damn the tea!' Mulholland all but shrieked. 'The explanation — now!'

'Very well,' Matthew relented. 'First of all, we've found the missing parish children.'

'We?'

'Doctor Carlyle, my wife — who is of course Doctor Carlyle's daughter — and myself.'

'Where?'

Matthew pointed to the newspaper article. 'There. In Limehouse. In that abandoned furniture warehouse.'

'Then why have you not brought them out to be reunited with their anxious parents?'

'That's the part I've shrunk from mentioning to anyone, including you,' Matthew admitted. 'They have cholera.'

Mulholland's eyes widened in shock and disbelief as he let that sink in. 'So they're condemned to die, is that what you're telling me?'

'No, not necessarily,' Matthew reassured him. 'Doctor Carlyle and his daughter are locked in there, with a police guard around the perimeter. They have all the essentials they need to minister to the children, of whom originally there were a dozen or so. They'd been enticed in there by a deserter from a circus that came through London a few weeks ago, a man whom the Met are urgently seeking. But it's believed that they drank contaminated water from the Limehouse Cut on the Regent's Canal, and contracted cholera. I don't profess any medical qualifications of my own, but Doctor Carlyle was of the opinion that if we kept them in strict isolation, so that they can't infect anyone else, then there was hope for some of them.'

'Only some of them?'

'Regrettably that's the case. We've already lost Bertie Jackson and Nicholas Wainwright, plus a young girl from another parish. But Adelaide tells me that one of those who was sick has made what promises to be a full recovery, so there must be hopes for the rest.'

'How can you communicate with her, if they're locked away in isolation?' Mulholland challenged him, and Matthew explained to him the intricate arrangements that had been made for food and other supplies to be brought in to those inside, at which times messages could be conveyed to those waiting outside. He also advised him of the three graves that already existed under the side wall of the factory forecourt, and how he had ensured that their occupants were interred with full Anglican rites, omitting to mention that this had been done some time after the actual burials.

Mulholland sat for some moments in deep thought, before looking back across at Matthew. 'I can now fully understand why you didn't feel that you could confide in me, but surely the parents have a right to know?'

'Of course they do, but what would be likely to happen if we advised them of the truth?'

'Clearly they'd want to be down there.'

'Obviously, but they wouldn't be allowed near their offspring, and if any news leaked out about the cholera that's raging inside, there'd be panic in the streets. It's difficult enough for us to maintain the arrangements we have at present, and would be next to impossible were we to invite the world and his wife to come and gawp, or for terrified idiots to write to the newspapers demanding that the place be burned down, with the children still inside.'

'I see your difficulty,' Mulholland conceded, 'and I agree that the parents shouldn't be informed yet, until we can be certain that the other children will survive. But you have to do something to quell this ridiculous story about ghosts and demons haunting the place.'

'I will, that I promise you, but I haven't yet had time to think of some plausible alternative explanation for what's going on down there.'

'Well, you'd better do so. And soon.' Then Mulholland's face softened and he reached across to take Matthew's hand. 'I realise what a severe ordeal this must be for you and the others, and I shall say prayers for your safe delivery, along with our precious parish children. Now I leave you in peace, but *please* do something — anything — to rescue your own reputation, and that of St Dustan's.'

Matthew found sleep impossible as he wrestled in his mind with one false explanation after another, and eventually he slid out of bed, made himself a couple of boiled eggs, then changed into fresh clothes and sat at the kitchen table waiting for the familiar sound of trundling coach wheels that indicated the arrival of the loyal Collins at his front door with the Carlyle coach. It was still fully dark as Collins swung the coach out of Church Lane into Oak Lane, then pulled sharply on the reins as he uttered a muted curse.

The entire length of Oak Lane was seemingly blocked in both directions with coaches, and to either side of the stationary conveyances were people scurrying on foot towards the gateway of the former Peebles factory yard, where they were being held back by Jennings's plain-clothed constables wielding billy clubs. Matthew jumped down from the coach, instructed Collins to make his way down Oak Lane whenever he could, then fought his way to the front of the loud demanding crowd in the gateway until he caught the eye of Jennings behind his line of men, urging them to remain vigilant and firm. Matthew waved, and he was able to lip-read Jennings's shouted command to allow Matthew through.

'A fine mess *you* created!' Jennings bellowed in Matthew's ear as he passed between two burly constables and into the yard. 'It's been like this since just before midnight, and the lads had me raised from my bed to deal with it. You owe Mrs Jennings a huge favour, not to mention an apology.'

'I assume that this mob outside were drawn down here by that shit in the evening paper?' Matthew demanded, and when Jennings growled his confirmation, Matthew assured him that his only contribution towards it had been to annoy its writer. 'If I catch up with Washbourne again, you'll be arresting me for wringing his scrawny neck!' Matthew assured him.

'And no doubt you'd be performing a great public service, and I for one would be looking the other way,' Jennings assured him, 'but until this baying crowd can be dispersed, we can't get any more supplies in. My wagons are halfway down the queue you must have passed on your way down the street.'

'Your billy clubs clearly aren't having the desired effect,' Matthew observed as he watched three of them raised in silent threat a few feet behind him, 'so what do you suggest?'

Jennings looked at him with a sick smirk. 'You created this mess, Reverend Devilslayer, so I suggest that you uncreate it.'

'And how do you propose that I do that?'

'Well, you're clearly the man of the hour — the great hero that they've all come to see in action — so go and tell them that there's nothing to see.'

'And would they be likely to believe me?'

'Who knows? But have you got any better suggestions?'

Since he didn't, Matthew turned back towards the crowd laying siege to the gateway and raised both arms in the air as he called for silence. When there was no obvious diminution in the volume, he took a deep breath and bawled at the top of his lungs, 'I'm Matthew West, the Demon Slayer! The man you've all come to see! Do you want to hear what I can tell you, or not?'

A few at the front of the crowd caught his words, and prevailed on the others to fall silent. Matthew seized the opportunity to shout some more. 'Because I can slay demons, I can tell you without reservation that there are none to be seen here, so you may as well go back to your homes.'

'So there *were* some, and you killed 'em?' demanded a man on the front row, and Matthew thought, *in for a penny, in for a pound*, as he shouted back, 'The evil in there departed at the first sight of me, and now we're turning it into consecrated ground.'

'Them graves down the side,' another man demanded, 'are they where you buried the demons?'

'Demons don't have material bodies, like you or I,' was Matthew's glib response. 'The people buried there are the unfortunate victims of the pestilence that resided here until I was called in to remove it.'

It went on like this for the best part of an hour, with Matthew deftly batting away one stupid question after another. He had the satisfaction of seeing the more gullible and prurient of his unwanted audience drifting away with disappointed mutters, followed by others who were not totally convinced, but who concluded that a good warm breakfast was preferable to standing out in the cold with nothing to see. Finally there was only one man left, and he smiled knowingly at Matthew.

'So Timmy Washbourne was writing his usual nonsense, that the case?'

'It most certainly is,' Matthew replied.

'But all that about turning a disused warehouse into consecrated ground was just some more nonsense of your own, wasn't it?' the man insisted.

'Who exactly are you?' Matthew demanded, and the man took out a notebook and pencil and gave him the benefit of a broad smile.

'I'm Edward Penrose, from *The Times*.'

'*The Times* newspaper?'

'The very same. Now, would you care to assist me in wrecking Timmy Washbourne's career?'

'I'd be more than delighted,' Matthew replied, 'but I can't let you in on the truth of what's going on here.'

'But you will eventually, if I assist you by writing something that will send Washbourne to the unemployment queue, and keep the crowds off your back?'

'Step inside,' Matthew invited him with a loud chuckle. 'This man's with me,' he instructed Jennings as he walked towards the line of his officers who were looking uncertainly down the rapidly emptying street, and beckoning forward the first of the police supply wagons.

'You're responsible for his every movement,' Jennings told him as he waved the first wagon into the yard, then trotted alongside it as it made its way towards the doors of the warehouse, which were opening slightly, with Adelaide's distinctive red hair visible under a makeshift bonnet as she peered out into what was now the half-light of a late dawn.

'Excuse me, just for a moment,' Matthew requested of Penrose as he scurried forward, calling out, 'Good morning, darling — sorry about the crowds earlier, but I'll explain in due course.'

'We have three more up and walking!' she called out triumphantly. 'And two of those we weren't sure about have shown signs of rallying.'

'How are you and your father?' he asked anxiously.

'We're both exhausted. And there's a new problem, I'm afraid. The children who're recovering have enormous appetites, and we're running out of food. To make matters worse, someone seems to be stealing it. We lost some cheese last night, along with two loaves of bread. It must be Jennings's men, so tell him to send us enough to feed his thieves as well.'

'I will do.'

'Got to go now,' she added as her face disappeared behind closed doors.

Matthew walked back to where Penrose had been watching, listening and taking notes. 'My wife,' Matthew told him.

'So why is she hiding from you?' was the question he both deserved and anticipated, and an idea began to form as he led the reporter slowly across the yard by his elbow, towards the line of graves. When they reached them, he nodded down at the ground.

'These are obviously not demons, but human beings. Or rather, they were. But the story behind how they come to be there would be worthy of a novel. And it will be exclusively yours, along with a lengthy interview with the most amazing, accomplished and beautiful woman in the world.'

'Your wife, I assume?'

'You assume correctly, and you have my word as a Man of God that no-one else will get that story, if you can come up with something that will keep the crowds away until it's time to tell the world what's really been happening here.'

Penrose tapped his nose thoughtfully with his pencil. 'The line about consecrated ground sounds half credible, particularly because you came out with it in public. Suppose we say that you're engaged in confidential arrangements to open a new church here? An extension to your existing one, which is St Dunstan's in Stepney, isn't it? Or was Washbourne lying about that as well?'

'No — but — well, look, you must keep this confidential, but I have my enemies even among my own congregation, and they've conspired to have me suspended from office as the parish curate, so please don't mention me in that regard.'

'All I really need from you is a firm denial that this place is haunted by devils, ghoulies and wicked beasties.'

'You can have that with the greatest of pleasure,' Matthew said. 'This place never was haunted by anything other than memories of its former days as a flourishing furniture warehouse. Tim Washbourne has it in for me, for two reasons. The first is that I made an idiot of him at a public meeting over a year ago now. And the second is that my sister rejected his advances.'

'Truly? Really, truly and absolutely?' Penrose enthused with a broad smile. 'I'd obviously love to be able to publish that, but if it's not true he could sue me and the newspaper for libel, so once again I need your word as a Man of God that it's true — the bit about your sister, that is.'

'Absolutely,' Matthew said.

In the distance St Mary's chimed ten o'clock, and Penrose put away his notebook and pencil. 'I have to go now, but look out for something in tomorrow's early edition. I'm really going to enjoy writing this!'

'Not half as much as I'll enjoy reading it,' Matthew beamed back. 'Power to your pencil, and I won't forget that exclusive interview with my wife.'

Penrose scurried away, almost cackling with glee, and Matthew wandered over to where Jennings was commanding the unloading of the final wagon for the morning.

'I hope you kept him in the dark,' Jennings muttered as Matthew approached, and was met with a broad grin.

'I actually sent him away to write something scurrilous about Timothy Washbourne.'

'So I don't need to have him arrested for crimes against the truth?'

'No, but you *must* stop your men stealing the food from the children's mouths,' Matthew insisted. 'It's reaching a critical stage in there, according to Adelaide, and they need all the food you're able to bring in.'

'That's not the first time you've made that accusation,' Jennings frowned, 'and I've grilled every one of them individually. They all swear black's white that they've not stolen so much as a piece of fruit, and I'm inclined to believe them. However, they *do* seem convinced that the building where they get the wood for their bonfires is haunted. They're big and brave when confronting lawbreakers, but a bit wobbly with ghosts, who they're blaming for the food thefts. But then, if they're ghosts, they don't need food, do they?'

'No,' Matthew agreed as he looked casually across at the tall tower that adorned the building in question. Then he thought he saw a vague shadow flit past a ventilation shaft of some sort at the top of the wall facing him, and he shuddered despite his religious beliefs. 'On the other hand,' he mused out loud, 'there may be a shadowy presence that needs to be fed.'

16

Carlyle reached down and felt the young boy's pulse, then asked him if he felt any pain. The boy shook his head, then looked up appealingly at Adelaide with one word: 'Water?' She handed him the cupful, which he drank down greedily, then asked for another. Three cups later he nodded, thanked her with his eyes and sank back onto his pallet.

'A good job we found enough cups in what must have been the former tenant's tearoom to give every child one each,' her father said, 'or else the infection would have gone through here like a forest fire. But his pulse is getting quite strong, and there doesn't seem to have been any bowel eruption for a little while, so that's one more category two ready to transfer to the category one list.'

Adelaide gave a little cheer from behind her rather bedraggled face mask. 'One more saved, thank God! One more who owes their life to you.'

'Not me — you,' Carlyle insisted. 'Haven't you realised yet that the boundary between life and death is walked constantly by the nurses? Or, in your case, the nurse. We doctors appear to do the clever stuff, and nurses bow and scrape to us on the wards, but then we walk away and leave the nurses to keep the patient alive.'

'I have to be totally honest and say that right now I'd rather be at home,' Adelaide sighed. 'I'm not sure I could stand being a fulltime nurse.'

'That's why we let nurses work only on regulated shifts,' her father reminded her. 'You've been at this for five days now, without a break. And I estimate that there'll be at least another week of this before we can say that the crisis is over. In the meantime, the hardest thing will be keeping those who've recovered from breaking out of here and making a run for home.'

'Can't we let them out, one by one, when they're ready?' Adelaide asked.

Carlyle shook his head. 'And what would happen when the first of them got home with the news? Every other parent would be down here, breaking down the doors. The category twos are still highly infectious, even if they seem to have survived within themselves. Never lose sight of that.'

'I suppose you're right,' Adelaide sighed, 'and nurses should never challenge a doctor's opinion, should they?'

Carlyle chuckled. 'You presumably read that in one of Florence Nightingale's books?'

'Yes, the one on practical nursing. I can only deeply admire her, for the way she battled on in far worse conditions that we have here, saving one soldier's life after another. But then she had no doctors to argue with, and her nurses did exactly what she told them, or else. She must have been quite a formidable lady in her day.'

'A bit like someone else I know,' Carlyle chuckled. 'And you talk as if she's dead now, when in fact she recently celebrated the thirtieth year of her nurses' training school inside St Thomas's, across the river. I was there at the event, and actually met her.'

'Really?' Adelaide asked, her eyes wide in wonder. 'What's she like?'

'Showing her age, as you'd expect,' her father replied. 'She's well into her seventies now, and a bit wobbly on her legs, in addition to having a bit of a stoop when she walks. But that hasn't softened her manner at all, and I distinctly remember the rude things she had to say about us doctors who don't give nurses the credit which they're due, although she did confide in me that she was in awe of my ability to open up human bodies and determine what they died of.'

'You actually spoke with her?'

'Of course — she spoke with all of us, around a table in one of the administrative offices in St Thomas's. She's not the Queen, you know.'

'I know that, but even so — I mean, she's such an accomplished lady.'

'And I'm *not* accomplished, you mean?'

'No, of course not. Just that — well, to have met her and everything. I'd give anything to be able to do that.'

At Matthew's request, Collins turned up with the coach shortly before six o'clock the following morning, and Matthew snuggled up tightly against the leather back rest inside as he fought against the intense cold of that early December morning. The traffic was light, and it was well before seven as Matthew strolled through the forecourt to the former Peebles warehouse towards the bonfire burning in front of the right-hand storage building.

Several constables murmured a greeting as he stood alongside them warming his hands, and one of them voiced their shared thought.

'You're here a bit early, aren't you?'

'Yes, but for a reason,' Matthew said. 'Would I be right in remembering something your Inspector once told me — that when you want to raid a house and find the person who occupies it at home, you do so shortly before dawn?'

'Yeah, why?'

Matthew nodded towards the tall building behind them. 'I thought I might try a spot of ghost hunting. Anybody fancy coming with me?'

It suddenly fell silent, and Matthew felt emboldened to underline his point. 'Food's going missing, right? None of you is responsible, or so you insist. You heard a man's cough from inside that building there, yes? And ghosts don't need to eat, or so I've been told. So work it out for yourselves — someone's inside there, stealing the food that my wife and her father are relying on to keep those children alive. So which of you brave boys is coming with me?'

The only response was a faint muttering, and nervous glances from one pair of eyes to another. Finally, one of them asked, 'What if it really *is* a ghost?'

'Well,' Matthew preened, 'since they reckon I'm the Demon Slayer, then who better qualified?'

He walked briskly away towards the storage building, mainly in order to get the circulation back into his toes, but also before common sense had the chance to overcome foolhardy bravado. The door had been left partly open, but it was pitch dark inside, and he halted just inside the doorway, in order to detect any sound there might be. It was deathly quiet — an unfortunate turn of thought, he reminded himself with a smile — and he picked his way carefully towards the centre of the ground floor, where he knew from memory the wood pile was located, although it had probably gone down considerably since Jennings's men had first found it.

He stopped suddenly when he realised that he was smelling something he should not be smelling. Wood smoke. He licked his index finger, then raised it in the air to check whether or not a breeze was wafting in the smell from the constables' fire outside, but that wasn't the case. Congratulating himself on the ‘sideways’ thinking that he was rapidly developing under his wife’s tutelage, he considered the alternatives, and looked all around him. Nothing. Nothing but a dull glow from somewhere above him that seemed to be diffusing through the entire building as the sun rose and began to cast its beam through one of the ventilation holes higher up the wall.

Then the realisation hit him. The only ventilation hole was on the side of the low tower that faced north-west, back towards Stepney, whereas the sun rose in the east. It was also barely seven o’clock on a dull December morning, and sunrise would not be until well after nine. So where was the glow coming from? Probably the same place as the smell of wood smoke, he concluded. Somewhere up there, someone had a fire going, and it was time to go back out and convince the constables that ghosts had no need to keep warm.

He heard the stealthy footfall less than a second before a blinding flash accompanied a crashing blow to the back of his head, and he slid, insensible, into the dust on the floor.

As luck would have it, Jennings opted to travel to the Limehouse detachment on the police wagon that was transporting the day shift. For once they were on time, and the weary outgoing nightshift gave a faint cheer as the wagon rumbled in, blowing hoar frost clouds across the courtyard with its wheels. The incoming men exchanged brief greetings with those who could now go home to their beds, and Jennings spoke briefly with the most senior man among those who were departing, John Daniels.

‘Nothing to report as usual, I suppose?’ he asked.

Daniels shook his head. ‘Quiet as a mouse, sir. Thanks for turning up on time, given that it’s so bloody cold this morning.

But your mate beat you to it — got here before daylight, so he must still be keen.'

'Who are you talking about?' Jennings asked, genuinely puzzled.

'That parson bloke — the one whose tasty-looking wife's working inside there.'

'Reverend West, you mean?'

'Yeah, that's him. He's gone ghost-hunting inside there,' Daniels told him, indicating the storage building with a jerk of the head. 'Mind you, he's been a while, so perhaps there are ghosts in there, after all.'

'What do you mean by "a while", exactly?'

'Well, at least a couple of hours, I reckon. It was fully dark when he went in.'

'And it never occurred to any of you to follow him in to make sure that he was all right?' Jennings demanded angrily.

Daniels shrugged, and looked down uneasily at the frozen ground. 'We're not employed to arrest ghosts, are we?'

'Right, you lot,' Jennings addressed the freshly arrived constables. 'You come with me, while you bunch of jessies from the night shift can stay on duty a while longer while we do the job you should have done before we even got here. Follow me, gentlemen.'

Jennings led the way to the door of the store building, six constables following a few paces behind. As they reached the door, Jennings drew his revolver and ordered his men to do the same. Then he edged forward and pushed the door fully open with the toe of his boot and crept in, his revolver in the standard upright position. The sight that confronted him in the watery light of a pale dawn left him gasping in fear.

Matthew came round to the sensation of aching shoulders and forearms, then realised that he was hanging in space. He looked up into the blazing bloodshot eyes of the man who was holding him in a vicelike grip by his wrists. As his eyesight cleared, Matthew noted with horror that the man who was holding him was himself hanging face down, his feet hooked over the bar of what looked like a circus trapeze, in some sort of sick re-enactment of the performance trick that had led to the death he had witnessed for himself some weeks ago now under the big top of Baxter's Circus.

'You die when I die,' the man holding him declared through blackened gums. 'They shoot me, then you fall like dirty Roberto.'

Matthew was vaguely aware of some sort of activity beneath his feet, but was unaware of how far down that was, or what would happen if, and when, he fell. He was dimly aware of Jennings speaking to someone, but all his focus was on how perilous his position was, suspended in mid-air, with only the hands of this seeming lunatic gripping his wrists and preserving him from a horrible death.

Thirty feet below him, Jennings sized up the situation and turned to two of his men, whispering an urgent instruction. 'Go and bring in one of those "life net" things that are lying out in the yard, while I keep this bugger talking. And make it a big one. Move your arses — now!'

The two men ran out of the building and retrieved the largest life net they could find. Meanwhile, Jennings had been conducting a shouted conversation with the upside down man hanging by his feet from the trapeze that he'd suspended from a bar that ran the width of the narrowing tower above them.

'I take it you're Giuseppe Rossi?' he shouted up, and the man yelled his reply.

'Yes. Giuseppe my name. Why you know me?'

'Did you kill Roberto, your partner in the circus act?'

'Yes. With happy. Roberto sex on my angel Luciana, give her *bambino*.'

At this point the two constables ran back in carrying the life net, and under Jennings's guidance they placed it as closely as possible in a direct vertical line with Matthew's dangling feet.

'Now what?' they asked of Jennings, who grinned sadistically.

'Now we open fire. Shoot high, and at all costs avoid hitting the parson. On my count of three…'

Matthew heard the three shots ring out, and felt his wrists coming free as he plummeted downwards. He made his peace with God in a microsecond, then instinctively arched his falling body into a horizontal angle at which to hit the ground, reasoning in a split second that seemed like an entire day that he could make his death instant if his spine was broken at the same time that his head hit the hard floor towards which he was hurtling. At all events, he would avoid the agony of fractured legs that poor Clarrie Hopgood had suffered.

He hit something solid, but not as hard as he had anticipated, and after a lightning prayer of thanks to God for making death so merciful he realised that he was flying back upwards, to what sounded like cheers. Wondering momentarily if this was the way everyone ascended to Heaven, he then found himself floating back down again, and as he looked down he saw the broken corpse of the man who had been holding him, crumpled up on the hard floor. Once again he hit the bottom and floated up, but not quite so far this time, and then he remembered the device from the yard outside that had bruised his ankle when they'd made their first cautious entry into the yard all those days ago.

He couldn't remember what Jennings had called it, but he recalled its purpose, so he forced himself back upright, ahead of the anticipated return to the bouncing platform that the parish children had used as a plaything. This time he came down feet first, but shot off the platform at a funny angle that pitched him into the rough stonework of the side wall. His face scraped down it, and this time when he reached ground level it was to the agony of a sprained ankle as he gave a yell of pain and rolled over into the dust.

Willing hands grabbed him and hauled him upright, and he found himself staring into the smiling face of John Jennings.

'Are you all right?' Jennings demanded anxiously.

Matthew replied groggily that he wasn't sure.

'Try walking,' Jennings instructed him as he took Matthew's armpit in his hand, and reduced his body weight as he tried his first tentative step, then sagged towards the floor with a yelp of pain. 'Try this,' Jennings instructed him as he threw Matthew's arm over his shoulder and helped him limp out of the building in an awkward one-legged fashion. They edged across the courtyard to where Collins had the coach waiting, and between them they lifted him inside, and Collins was instructed to deliver Matthew back to Stepney, and call a doctor.

Adelaide was standing at the partly open doorway of the main building, watching the entire proceedings, and she called out in alarm to Jennings. 'We heard gun shots — is Matthew all right?'

'Perfectly,' Jennings replied. 'But let's just say that he failed his first circus audition. Don't expect to see him again for a day or two.'

17

'Come in, the door's unlocked!' Matthew bellowed from where he sat in his favourite armchair in Curate's House, his injured ankle tightly bandaged and resting out in front of him on a footstool where the doctor had insisted that he keep it. The fire that Collins had insisted on lighting had almost gone out, and whoever this visitor was, Matthew hoped that they would consent to bringing in more wood from the stack at the kitchen door. Then he abandoned that thought when he saw that his visitor was Mulholland.

'How are you coming along?' the vicar asked in his best pastoral 'sick visiting' voice.

Matthew smiled. 'The doctor says I'll live, provided that I do what I'm told. Which is something I've got very used to since I got married.'

'This might cheer you up,' Mulholland replied as he handed over that morning's copy of *The Times*, opened at the third page.

Matthew took the newspaper from him and began to read, chuckling more and more loudly as he read what Penrose had written as promised. Not only had he advised his readers that the rumours of ghostly happenings in and around the abandoned furniture warehouse in Limehouse were completely untrue, but he had added that they were a prime example of the 'irresponsible, morally corrupt and professionally inexcusable balderdash' dreamed up in the sick mind of a 'clearly mentally disturbed so-called journalist called Timothy Washbourne, who must be regarded as a disgrace to the profession which he hopefully will not be following for much longer.'

Penrose had gone on to describe how he had met with 'a most pleasant and worthy representative of the established Church, the Reverend Matthew West from St Dunstan's parish in Stepney,' who had assured him that his presence in Limehouse was in connection with a planned outreach centre from his parish that would be based on the former warehouse site. 'It is to be regarded as one of God's blessings,' Penrose had concluded, 'that parishes in our East End have such dedicated Men of God who can move among us and protect us, not from non-existent ghosts, demons and evil entities, but raving lunatics such as Timothy Washbourne, whose only real connection with the worthy Reverend is that his sister — quite rightly — rejected his sweaty advances, further demonstrating with what good taste the West family is imbued.'

Matthew realised that he was chuckling so hard that he was making his ankle hurt, and he looked up at Mulholland with a triumphant grin. 'Will that do for the time being?' he asked.

Mulholland nodded. 'More than adequately. Now, what can I do for our "pleasant and worthy" parish champion? Beatrice has baked some scones, and they're on the kitchen table, if you can hobble that far once I put the kettle on. I'll be back later with your dinner, and are there any books that I can lend you from my humble library?'

'Thank you most sincerely for feeding me,' Matthew replied warmly. 'But as you rightly deduce, my mobility is a little restricted at the moment, so there *is* something you can help me with.'

'Gladly. What is it?'

'I'm dying for a pee, so could you help me hobble upstairs?'

Mulholland wasn't Matthew's only visitor that day. The sun was beginning to set through the living room window that faced west as the knock on the door was followed almost immediately by the sound of it being opened, and Jennings calling down the hall. He followed Matthew's answering shout, and came into the living room with a frown.

'Your security's rubbish. Anyone could walk in here and take advantage of your current indisposition.'

'Like you just did, you mean?'

'Do you want this lamb roast supper or not?' Jennings joked back. 'I'll put it on the kitchen table through there, shall I?'

'You shall, then you can help me walk in there and eat it. I don't have a very big appetite at the moment, and the vicar's wife seems convinced that I have an army hidden inside here.'

'Thank you for saving my life, by the way,' Matthew said between mouthfuls of roast lamb with potatoes and carrots in gravy. 'That *was* George Ross, I take it, and you *did* kill him?'

'I did indeed,' Jennings replied, 'since mine was the shot that went through his head. Bentinck managed to shoot him in the arse, and we never did find out where Langton's bullet went. But yes, he's as dead as we need him to be.'

'And I seem to recall that he confessed to killing Roberto? Pardon my vagueness, but I was contemplating a messy death at the time.'

'Enough for me, anyway, and my men can corroborate it. I saved the community the cost of a trial.'

'You also deprived a woman of her husband, and a daughter of her father,' Matthew reminded him.

Jennings made a rude noise. 'Always the bloody parson. But presumably you enjoyed your little play on the toy?'

'Yes, thank you for that as well,' Matthew nodded. 'And for this delicious dinner. You aren't by any chance looking for a living-in position for a month, are you?'

'You don't have a month,' Jennings told him. 'That's why I'm really here, with a message for you from Carlyle. He reckons that the children will all be ready to leave within a week, if they haven't broken out of there already. I think he's having problems keeping the fully fit ones confined.' Matthew's face fell, and Jennings looked puzzled. 'Why the glum face? Isn't that good news?'

'In one sense, yes,' Matthew replied. 'But what about the parents whose children *won't* be coming out of there alive? I've been dreading this moment for some time — having to break the bad news to some parents, as well as the good news to the rest.'

'Comes with your job, I suppose,' Jennings mused, 'but I know what you mean. The part of my job that I find the hardest is telling some poor woman with five children and a leaking roof that she's now a widow.'

'How do you do it?' Matthew asked.

Jennings shrugged. 'I do it, that's all.'

'Talking of wives deprived of husbands, was there any message from Adelaide?'

'There was,' Jennings admitted with a smirk, 'but I'd be too embarrassed to repeat it. Let's just say that her homecoming will be both joyful and somewhat physical.'

'Tell her that I'll be back in two days at most.'

'I will, of course, but are you sure you will?'

'Depend upon it. I'll need her advice on how to break the news about the dead ones.'

'Surely clergymen like yourself are trained to do that sort of thing?'

'Not "trained", Inspector. We somehow learn how to do it as we go along. We're not as all powerful as some people seem to think. There are limits to our talents, as you're about to discover.'

'Meaning?'

'Meaning that I can only hobble around on one leg, and even then only with the aid of that walking stick. There are restrictions when you have one hand firmly grasping a walking stick.'

'I'm here to help,' Jennings unwisely offered.

A broad smile lit Matthew's face. 'The axe is under the kitchen porch, and the woodpile's on the grass to the side. You'll find the coal bucket by the living room fire, and thank you most sincerely for your offer.'

'Matthew, are you sure you should be attempting to walk so soon?' Mulholland asked solicitously as he opened the vicarage front door. 'Thank you for bringing back my wife's food bowls, but you really shouldn't have. I could have collected them on my next visit.'

'That's not why I'm here,' Matthew replied gloomily. 'I have good news and bad news, I'm afraid.'

'Has something happened to the children?' Mulholland asked in hushed tones as he and his wife sat opposite Matthew in the living room into which he'd been invited.

'Yes — that's the good news,' Matthew hastened to reassure them. 'They can be allowed back home in a week or so's time.'

'What's so gloomy about that?' Mulholland asked as his wife clapped her hands daintily together and muttered thanks to God.

'What do I tell the parents of the others?' Matthew asked, almost in tears at the very prospect.

Mulholland's face fell. 'I see what you mean. Would you like me to do it? I mean, you've done — and suffered — enough already.'

'No, it's something I feel I must do,' Matthew insisted, 'but I'd dearly welcome your advice on how exactly to do it.'

Mulholland sat deep in thought for a moment, then gave his conclusion. 'A good number of the parishioners have been enquiring about your absence from parish duties of late. I clearly haven't given any reason, but it would be an appropriate answer to all their enquiries were you to hold a meeting in the church hall and explain where you've been for the past two weeks. Then you can break the news that you've managed to locate their children, that some of them are alive and well, but that unfortunately there are some who didn't make it.' He saw the distress in Matthew's face and reached out to take his hand. 'It's asking a great deal of anyone, but I know that your faith is deep, and your commitment strong, and we can be assured that God will give you the strength.'

'And, of course, I won't be doing it in my capacity as curate, will I?' Matthew pointed out bitterly.

Mulholland's fervent gaze dropped to the carpet. 'I'm sorry, Matthew, but I've already explained my position on that more than once.'

'Of course,' Matthew confirmed, 'and please excuse my childishness. It's just that I feel so utterly alone and deserted at this precise moment.'

It fell silent until Mulholland said quietly, 'Imagine how our Lord must have felt, hanging on the Cross at Golgotha. But his Father rescued him.'

'Not until he'd suffered for the best part of a day,' Matthew reminded him as he gave way to a shudder. 'I can only hope to be half as brave.'

A tear rolled down Adelaide's face as she looked out through the half-open door and saw Matthew leaning on his walking stick and looking hopefully in her direction. 'Thank God!' she called out in a voice gurgling with emotion. 'I nearly died when I saw you being led out of that building next door!'

'I nearly died while I was in there,' Matthew joked back. 'I never want to see another circus for as long as I live. But Rossi's dead.'

'I know, Jennings told Father. Are you *sure* that you only have that broken leg?'

'It's only a sprained ankle,' Matthew reassured her, 'and even that feels better for seeing you again. The house is in a bit of a mess, I'm afraid.'

'You should see inside here!' she chuckled ruefully. 'I'll need some more clean drawers before we leave here, so how do you feel about attracting giggles from sales ladies when you buy me some more?'

Matthew laughed out loud. 'I'll pretend that they're for my mistress, but I'll remember to ditch the dog collar first. When do you plan to release your hostages?'

'Father reckons next Tuesday — that gives us just under a week. How do you suggest we do it? Let them out here, and let the parents collect them, or organise for them to be taken back up to St Dunstan's?'

'Don't know yet, but leave that with me. Can you be certain of Tuesday as the day?'

'As certain as Father is, anyway.'

'Are there any more dead?'

'No, thank God. They're all out of immediate danger, but we have to wait until the ones who were near death when we first got here have progressed to the stage at which they're no longer infectious. That's why we have to wait until Tuesday.'

'Are you going to stay out there all day?' came a man's voice from just behind her, and Carlyle's face appeared in the doorway with a broad grin on it. 'Go away, and stop bothering my daughter,' he jested.

An idea had begun to form in Matthew's mind as he walked across to where Jennings was talking to his police team around the bonfire. As he lurched level with them, Jennings turned in his direction, looked pointedly at his shoulder and asked, 'What happened to your parrot?' Two of his men sniggered, and Matthew was tempted to threaten to batter Jennings to death with his walking stick, but refrained when he realised that he needed his co-operation.

'How many police coaches can you make available? The sort that you transport prisoners in, not the open-sided things that look like dung carts?'

'Depends what you need them for.'

'When the children are released next Tuesday, I was thinking that perhaps they might appreciate a ride back to Stepney in real police vehicles. They have to get back somehow or other, and not all their families have coaches at their disposal.'

'I suppose I could arrange it, given that it will mark the end of one of the worst jobs I've ever been on,' Jennings conceded grudgingly. 'We could call it a celebration parade.'

'Excellent,' Matthew said. 'I'll let you know precisely when it's to happen, but I'll be elsewhere at the time.'

Mulholland nodded his approval at the idea, and agreed that on balance it was perhaps the most humane way that things might be organised. 'But won't you need to be down there, organising things at that end?' he asked, in response to which Matthew shook his head.

'My place is here, when the children arrive. Particularly for the parents of those who won't. I've written out what I'd like you to tell the parishioners at the morning and evening services on Sunday, and of course I'll need the use of the church hall at around dinner time on Tuesday.'

During both sermons on the following Sunday, the vicar announced to a stunned congregation that the Reverend West had organised a meeting in the church hall for midday on Tuesday, when he would have tidings to impart regarding the missing parish children.

The news spread like a forest fire throughout the parish, and at the appointed time Matthew was waiting inside the hall, having returned an hour earlier from Limehouse, where he'd confirmed the last-minute details, and ensured that everything was in hand. He said a silent prayer, asking God for the strength to do what he had to do, then when satisfied that all the relevant parents were present, talking softly and nervously among themselves, he rose to his feet. He had expected to have to call for silence, but he got that instantly once he cleared his throat nervously, and began, hoping that he'd timed his address accurately.

'You've probably all wondered where I've been for the past few weeks,' he choked, then took time to clear the nervous mucus from his throat, apologised, and continued. 'I've actually been a few miles away from here, in the search for your missing children, and I'm delighted to say that I found them.'

He paused for the gasps of delight to ripple through his audience, and when the first anxious questions were shouted up from the seats in front of him, he raised his hand and asked to be allowed to finish before he answered any of them.

'I can't take all the credit, since I was joined by some very special and dedicated people, including my own wife, her father, and a detective inspector from Scotland Yard. We found the children, but they had previously been captured by a wicked man who I am glad to say has been brought to justice, and some of them were very ill. Doctor Carlyle and his daughter have devoted the best part of two weeks to preserving as many of their lives as was humanly possible, but I regret to have to advise you that there were three from this parish that they couldn't save.'

He'd braced himself mentally for the reaction, but even so he all but wilted under the barrage of agonised cries for him to name the dead ones, grimly sticking to the plan he'd devised for breaking the bad news as easily as possible. He silently prayed to God for forgiveness for prolonging their agony, and for the strength to keep going until the coaches arrived with the survivors.

'Let us raise our voices in prayer, and our hearts in joyous thanks for the merciful God who has extended His loving arm to protect so many of our precious children,' he pleaded loudly as he launched into a rendition of the Lord's Prayer that he dragged out for as long as he could, before reading from Isaiah, Chapter 40, Verse 1, 'Comfort ye, comfort ye my people, saith your God', and plodding on doggedly until a few eyes opened as their owners looked up at him, wondering at the obvious delay. Suddenly, to his intense relief, he heard the rumble of the first coach wheels on the long drive up to the church and pronounced the 'Amen,' before smiling down at his flock.

'I do believe that our beautiful children have returned,' he announced, then stepped back hastily as the frantic rush for the doors threatened to knock him backwards.

He followed the shrieks and wails of joy outside, and stood slightly back from it all, as parents crushed children to their chests, calling out loud praises to God, and children cried their lungs out, assuring their rapturous mothers and fathers that they were fully recovered, and promising never to leave home ever again. Then his heart sank as he saw three couples, their shoulders shaking in grief, walking resignedly towards him, and he prayed like never before.

'Bertie didn't survive, did he?' Mrs Jackson said.

Jim Wainwright had only one question that he kept repeating over and over. 'Why did God take our Nicky?' he pleaded as tears rolled down his weathered face. 'He was such a good boy, really.'

Matthew stepped forward and raised his hands above their heads as they stood sobbing before him, muttering prayers of consolation and calling down blessings on the bereaved. Eventually his own voice gave out as it was drowned in his own vicarious grief for what these decent people must be suffering, and as he saw them shuffling back towards their homes it was through a river of tears of his own. He looked up as a hand was outstretched towards him, and he found himself looking through the veil of his misery at the face of Thomas Mulholland.

'We give frequent blessing to others in their hour of suffering,' the vicar said quietly, 'but who blesses us when our time of need draws nigh?' He placed his hand down firmly on Matthew's head, and in a voice quivering with emotion of his own, he said, 'God Bless you, my brother in Christ.'

Matthew was awoken from the depth of his distraction by a familiar voice, and looked towards where it was coming from. Another coach was rolling into place at the end of the queue of coaches in the long driveway, and long before it came to a halt there was a flurry of feathered bonnet and a flash of faded blue costume as Adelaide leaped from the open door and ran towards him, oblivious of the crowd that she had to dodge through on her way. She all but bowled Mulholland aside as she flung herself on Matthew with shrieks of delight, and threatened to stop his breathing with a long kiss that drove all the wind out of him.

He looked down at her, searching for the words. Eventually, he said simply, 'Welcome back to St Dunstan's, Mrs West.'

'I hope you mean that,' she gurgled. 'I'm going straight inside for a long bath that I've been dreaming of for two weeks.'

18

'We don't realise how much we take things for granted until they're denied us,' Adelaide said as she sat by the fire, dressed in a long, padded dressing gown and drying her hair with a fresh towel. 'Like being able to take a bath whenever you wish, or simply being able to go for a walk. All that time cooped up in that dreadful warehouse place, I came to realise how prisoners must feel. Then to be allowed out, and into a coach — well, it was just so *liberating*. I think I might join some organisation that helps to bring comfort to prisoners locked up for crimes that they didn't commit — you *do* hear of such things, don't you?'

'Particularly from those prisoners themselves,' Matthew replied cynically. 'I never heard of one yet who wasn't claiming to be innocent, and you have to remember that most of those miserable wretches inside our gaols actually *did* commit crimes — some of them very brutal. Stick to nursing.'

'But I'm not a nurse,' Adelaide objected.

Matthew raised both eyebrows in argument. 'Really? What would you call what you did inside that warehouse? I bet if I were to ask the parish children who you helped through their cholera to describe what you did for them, they'd use the word nurse in every sentence.'

'But that wasn't proper nursing, was it? Just sitting by them and holding their hands, assuring them that they were going to get well soon, and could go home then. Giving them cups of water, and occasionally wiping up their — well, you know what I mean.'

'And how does Florence Nightingale define nursing?' Matthew argued.

Adelaide had to admit that he had a point. 'It was reading her books that inspired me to keep going, as it happens. Every night, when I had a few minutes to myself, I read what she'd written. She's probably the most remarkable woman I've ever encountered, or at least read about. You're right that her idea of nursing is making the patient feel as happy and healthy as you can, while making sure that everything around them is clean and orderly, and that the doctor's instructions are followed to the letter. Which makes it even more remarkable when you read her other book, in which she tells women that they must strive to be their best, and not simply and meekly accept the roles allocated to them by men.'

Matthew chuckled. 'No wonder you enjoyed reading what she'd written. She was writing about you!'

'Nonsense,' Adelaide protested. 'I could never be the woman she is, even though I agree with everything she wrote. Look at what she achieved, and is *still* achieving, with her nurses' training in St Thomas's Hospital. Perhaps if I could learn under her tutelage, I might consider nursing as a profession after all.'

'And what would your father's reaction be, losing his assistant? His right hand person?'

She frowned. 'There's always that, of course, although he assures me that he won't need me for the rest of this week. He says that I'm entitled to a few days of rest, and I'm going to take him up on that, and make the best of it. Apart from looking after you, of course — how's your ankle coming on?'

'It's got a lot better now that I don't have to hobble around that dreadful courtyard in Limehouse, but I'm feeling guilty that we abandoned those four graves. Someone needs to find out where Jenny Savage lived, and contact her parents.'

'You could ask Inspector Jennings to do that, surely? But if it'll make you feel better, why don't you do something to create a memorial garden or something down there? You know, proper gravestones and things?'

'It's not our land, for one thing,' Matthew reminded her. 'I just hope that whoever takes over that property honours what we've done, and doesn't go digging up the bodies, or something horrible like that.'

'Couldn't the parish acquire it? Using money from the Poor Fund?' She saw his face cloud over, and put her hand to her mouth. 'Oh, I'm *so* sorry — I just didn't think.'

'You did, though,' Matthew said reassuringly, 'and it's given me an idea. I'll go and sound out the vicar tomorrow, but right now we need to be thinking about supper. Do you want Mrs Bentley's leek and ham pie, or Mrs Vane's turnip pasties?'

Since earlier that day there'd been a constant stream of mothers at their door, bearing culinary expressions of thanks for bringing their offspring back safely, and it seemed unlikely that they'd need to do any cooking until the weekend, if this kept up.

Adelaide thought for a moment, then smiled. 'Let's have the pasties, and you can peel and boil the potatoes while I continue to play the lady of leisure. Then you can tell me how much you love me.'

The following morning Matthew was admitted into the vicarage by a smiling Beatrice Mulholland, who thanked him for the excuse to put the pot on to boil and get rid of some more of her cheese scones. Her husband rose from his desk and gestured for Matthew to take one of the comfortable chairs in the centre of his study, while he came from behind his desk to occupy the other. He listened attentively to Matthew's suggestion that the parish do something to acquire the land in Limehouse in which three of their parish were buried, and promised to make enquiries. Then he got back up, took a piece of paper from his desk, and handed it to Matthew.

'I take it that this name is familiar to you, since I believe that he wrote that piece for *The Times* that cleared your name.'

Matthew looked at the name 'Edward Penrose' and the telephone number, and nodded.

'He telephoned here yesterday, asking that you get in contact with him,' Matthew was told. 'He claims that you owe him the benefit of an interview with him, and I promised that you'd be in touch. There's a telephone up there on my desk; please feel free to use it, and if this Mr Penrose agrees to write something more about the miracles performed by your wife and father-in-law, you might mention that we're thinking of creating a permanent memorial down there, and invite the public to make donations.'

Thanking him most profusely, and after being given a brief lesson in how telephones worked, Matthew found himself making arrangements for Penrose to call at Curate's House for dinner the following day, at which he could meet with Adelaide and ask her whatever questions he wished.

'I knew I had a reason for saving the leek and ham pie,' Adelaide said when he returned home with the news, 'and since I only came across one tiny bit of potato peel on my plate yesterday, you can do the honours again.'

The following day felt like the most civilised either of them had experienced for some time, as they welcomed a smiling Penrose into their home, and plied him with tea, leek and ham pie and assorted cooked vegetables. Then they set about telling each of their versions of events as they had occurred, including the unfortunate death of the man responsible for enticing the children away in the first place when he tried to evade police who were seeking him on an unrelated murder charge. Adelaide waxed lyrical about the inspiration she'd drawn from the writings of Florence Nightingale, and how she felt sure that strict adherence to what the woman had written about practical nursing had been what had pulled nine of the dozen or so St Dunstan's children through a virulent outbreak of cholera.

'I hope he doesn't concentrate on what I told him about Rossi's death,' Matthew reflected after they'd shown him out in the middle of the afternoon with an assurance that they'd purchase a copy of the following morning's paper.

'Why not?' Adelaide queried. 'After all, what you did was heroic.'

'As you once observed,' Matthew reminded her, 'heroes are merely men with no imagination. What I did was foolhardy.'

'It was also brave,' she insisted. 'But I agree that you're given to bouts of impetuosity that are inclined to get you into trouble.'

'It was impetuosity that led to my proposing marriage to you,' he reminded her.

She shook her head. 'As I recall, you tricked *me* into proposing to *you*. And look what trouble *that* got me into.'

'Is that a formal complaint?'

'Far from it. After a heavy dinner like that, do you think we'll need any supper?'

'Probably not, why?'

'How "early" can an early night be?'

'It's not even four o'clock yet!' Matthew protested.

Adelaide smiled as she pulled him to her. 'See how much trouble you cause me? Upstairs, now.'

They had barely finished breakfast the following morning when there came an urgent hammering on their front door, which upon investigation proved to have come from Joseph Mulholland, who was waving a copy of that morning's *Times* newspaper in their faces.

'You're both famous!' he exclaimed. 'And I've already had a telephone call from some stonemasonry business, all but begging to be allowed to install headstones free of charge in the memorial garden! Well done, both of you! I have to go about my business, but read this and enjoy your morning!'

They eagerly spread the lengthy article under Edward Penrose's by-line down on the kitchen table and read it, Matthew doing so over Adelaide's shoulder as he occasionally broke off to kiss the top of her head. It was not only a very accurate summary of the circumstances that had led to the parish children being trapped inside the deserted furniture warehouse by cholera, and the fact that only three of the Stepney children had died. However, it was a beautifully crafted piece about the 'Angel of Limehouse, Adelaide West', and how she had been inspired by the teachings and example of Florence Nightingale to employ the best nursing practices alongside her dedicated surgeon father, who had prescribed the regimes that slowly and painstakingly restored the sick children to full health. It concluded with mention of the proposed memorial garden, and a request for public donations towards it.

'So now you're officially an angel,' Matthew teased Adelaide, then stepped back with concern when he saw the tears rolling down her face. 'Why did that upset you?' he asked. 'It was beautifully written.'

'That's why I'm crying,' Adelaide said as she reached into the sleeve of her blouse for a handkerchief. 'It's so lovely, and I just felt the tears welling up and overcoming me. I'm sorry, you must think me a real mimsy.'

'You certainly seem to have softened since we got married,' Matthew agreed. 'And yet on other occasions you've lost control in exactly the opposite direction, and all but exploded with anger.'

'I think I need to consult Father about that,' Adelaide agreed with a coy smile, 'and don't forget that I'll be going back to work at the hospital on Monday.'

19

When Monday morning came, and Adelaide headed off for the mortuary, clearly eager to be getting back to work, Matthew took as long as he could washing up the breakfast dishes, then sat forlornly at the kitchen table, reading his Bible. He reflected sadly on his own lack of any sense of purpose, given his suspension from parish duties. As events had transpired, it had been as well that he had been relieved of them during the two weeks or so in which he'd been making the daily journey down to Limehouse, but now the reality sank in. He kept turning the pages of his Bible at random, almost ashamed to be indulging in the old wives' practice that was allegedly the means of receiving a message direct from God.

Then he froze when he looked down at the passage that had fallen into view as he turned the well-worn leaves for the fifth time. It was from Jeremiah 29:11, and it read: 'For I know the plans I have for you, declares the Lord, plans to prosper you and not to harm you, plans to give you hope and a future.'

Almost instantly came a knock on the front door, and Matthew rose hastily and limped down the hall to answer it, half expecting to find St Peter himself on his doorstep. Instead it was Joseph Mulholland, sporting an unaccustomed broad smile.

'Such news, Matthew — may I come in?'

Matthew nodded unenthusiastically, and stepped back into the hall to grant the vicar admission, then led the way into the kitchen and put the pot on to boil for tea. Mulholland was clearly at bursting point with the good news that he claimed to be bearing, so Matthew put on a brave encouraging smile and invited him to unburden himself.

'We have the land for the memorial garden in Limehouse! I received a telephone call only a few minutes ago, from the property company that owns the land. They read that wonderful piece in *The Times*, and wish to portion off the right hand side of the forecourt in front of the warehouse, which I believe is where the graves are located. What's more, they're prepared to convey it to us for nothing in return for a suitable acknowledgment. We already have that offer of free headstones, of course, so we can go ahead whenever you're ready!'

'We'll need to plant turf, and install suitable pots and things for flowers,' Matthew replied, 'but I'd be happy to organise a working party from the parish. We have several gardeners among our congregation, I seem to recall, and it'll give me something to occupy my time.'

'Could you also prepare some sort of dedication service, with a suitable sermon and appropriate hymns?' Mulholland asked.

Matthew nodded. 'Of course, but I imagine that you'd like to prepare your own. I assume that you'll be conducting the service?'

'That's the other great news, Matthew! I can now officially reinstate you as Curate, and may I say how much my heart overflows with joy at being able to do so?'

Matthew's jaw dropped, and he seemed incapable of responding, so Mulholland continued.

'Late yesterday afternoon I received a visit from Edgar Holroyd. He seemed very furtive, and almost embarrassed to be calling on me, but he eventually blurted out that his conscience was weighed down with guilt about the secret he'd been keeping.'

'If it's about the children being imprisoned in Limehouse, it's a bit late to be telling us that,' Matthew growled.

Mulholland raised his hand. 'Let me finish, please! This was something else entirely — a conversation he'd overheard between his parents. It seems that after you left their house, having — according to them — all but accused poor Edgar of some crime or other, they decided to take their revenge by setting you up so that you appeared to have been stealing collection money. It was agreed that his father Thomas would extract a sum from the total, using the key that you normally lend him to open the strongbox, then leave it on the altar for you to find. His wife was then to arrange to be in the church and see you with it in your hand.'

'I knew it!' Matthew said. 'Edgar finally came good!'

'He certainly did. It seems that he couldn't live with what he knew after what you did for him, and how you and Adelaide saved so many of his friends. It must have taken great courage for him to come forward like that and expose his parents to accusations of such dishonesty.'

'Have you spoken with them?'

'Indeed I have — late yesterday evening. I took Edgar back with me, told them what a wonderful young man they'd raised, blessed with the purity of heart of our Lord, then demanded why they should wish to plot against the best curate this parish has ever had. They both confessed on the spot — in fact, the wife was on her knees, pleading for forgiveness and begging for some penance that she might be given in order to expiate her sin. So I removed her from the flower roster, which is all the authority I had over her. She was also instructed to read her Bible in order to remind herself of what our Lord suffered in order that good men like you might be inspired to devote their lives to others.'

'And her husband?'

'Thomas Holroyd is no longer one of our sidesmen, so you might wish to select another one before the Sunday morning service, which I'd be obliged if you'd take. Now, just to celebrate your resumption of duties, and to prove how much courage and fortitude you're capable of demonstrating in the face of peril, here are some of Beatrice's coconut macaroons.'

There were almost a hundred people gathered, heads bowed, and tears on most faces, as Matthew swallowed hard himself and forced out the words, 'Suffer little children.' The sun had chosen to glisten the frost on the freshly laid turf around the three graves, now with suitable headstones bearing inscriptions, and it seemed to bring a glow to the green chasuble he'd donned for the occasion, while Adelaide, standing proudly by his side, could have sworn that there was a halo above his head, although it might have been the sunlight reflecting off the polished tombstones that was partly blinding her eyes.

Towards the rear of the group stood Edward Penrose, occasionally jotting down notes, but for most of the time looking anxiously out towards the gateway that led in from Oak Lane. The service had just come to an end, and the long queue had just begun to move forward to lay flowers on the graves, including the immediate family of Jenny Savage from the nearby parish of Southwark, when Penrose allowed himself a smile and walked forward to meet the coach that had just turned into the yard.

He glanced across at Adelaide, who seemed to be occupied in standing alongside Matthew and giving words of comfort to those who were laying flowers, then stood by to welcome the visitor he had invited to attend. Then he called loudly to

Adelaide, who frowned, said something to Matthew, then walked over to where Penrose was standing with an elderlylady at the door to what was presumably her carriage.

'Adelaide, this lady asked most solicitously to be allowed to meet you. This is Adelaide West, madam. Adelaide, please say hello to Miss Florence Nightingale.'

The words hit her like a blow to the head, and for a moment she felt as if she was about to swoon. Then she broke into a wide grin, and took the gloved hand that was held out to her, not sure whether or not it might be appropriate to curtsy.

'I'm *so* honoured!' she gasped.

Florence shook her head. 'Indeed, it is I who am honoured, to have been spoken about so graciously by someone whose dedication to my lifelong teachings was so gratifying.'

'I was inspired by them,' Adelaide blurted, 'and I agreed with every word you wrote. Oh, please excuse me, I didn't intend that to sound so arrogant.'

'It did not — it merely confirmed an idea in my head.'

'But surely you don't need people like me to assure you that what you say about the practicalities of nursing is correct — it's so obvious to anyone who takes the time to read your words, and who has any experience of the realities of the profession.'

'You consider it a profession?' Florence asked with the hint of a conspiratorial smile.

'Of course, as anyone would,' Adelaide confirmed.

'And would you like to join that profession?'

Adelaide allowed herself a modest smile. 'Forgive me, but after my experiences down here at Limehouse, I'm not sure that I possess the stamina.'

Florence laughed lightly. 'Very few young ladies do. But you have the spirit, and you have clearly embraced my philosophies regarding nursing. I wish to invite you to pass them on to others.'

'I'm not sure I understand you,' Adelaide replied with a furrowed brow, but Florence had clearly come prepared with a little speech.

'As you may know, I have a nursing school in St Thomas's Hospital, from which groups of nurses are sent to other hospitals around the nation, but particularly here in London. It is imperative that both before they leave for these outposts, and by way of regular reinforcement while they are there, they are reminded of the discipline that nursing demands. Scrupulously clean wards, attention to statistics and record keeping, obedience to doctors' instructions and so on. I wish you to take up a position working under me to ensure that this happens, since you have the ideal qualifications. Your father is a surgeon, you have practical experience in nursing under impossible conditions, and you seem to have both absorbed and adopted my philosophies.'

Adelaide's mouth finally returned from the gaping that had accompanied all this, and she looked wildly across to where Matthew appeared to have just finished consoling the last of the mourners. She called out loudly to him, then waved for him to join her. 'Matthew,' she explained breathlessly as she grasped his hand, 'this lady is Florence Nightingale! Miss Nightingale has offered me a job working alongside her.'

'She has, provided that you learn to call her "Florence", but do I detect that you intend to accept?' Florence asked eagerly.

Adelaide began to nod enthusiastically, then something occurred to her, and she looked back pleadingly. 'Could we possibly delay it by, perhaps, a year?'

'Of course, but why?' Florence asked, just before Matthew made his own point.

‘Surely your father could find someone else to replace you sooner than that?’

‘It’s not that,’ Adelaide said warmly as she hugged him to her. ‘I should have told you earlier, but I’ve been waiting for the right moment, and this would seem to be it. I now know why I’ve been getting so emotional recently. I’m carrying our first child, and before June of next year you’ll need to be taught more than how to boil an egg.’

A NOTE TO THE READER

Dear Reader,

Thank you for taking the time to join Matthew, Adelaide, Carlyle and Jennings in their latest encounter with the seedier side of late Victorian London. Although the events depicted were of course fictional, they were, as ever, based on solid historical facts — facts which on occasions threaten to rival the fiction.

The Parish of St Dunstan's in Stepney still exists, and is proud of its one thousand year history since its foundation by St Dunstan himself, who at the time was the Bishop of London, while also being the Lord of the Manor of Stepney. The first stone church on the site dates back to the Tenth Century, when it was known as 'The Mother Church of the East End', until population growth led to the creation of 'daughter' parishes. The building featured in this novel would have been the third one on the site, built in the fifteenth century, and sadly in need of the restoration that occurred a few years later.

The rapid population growth that made St Dunstan's too small for its congregation also led to the slum ghettos for which the East End of London soon became famous. Chief among these was Limehouse, and if residents of its modern manifestation as part of Tower Hamlets were offended by my description of it, then they should engage in the same research that I did. In 1894, Limehouse was a festering sore on the north bank of the Thames, reaping the whirlwind of its maritime industrialisation in the form of tenement slums whose residents lived a hand-to-mouth existence surrounded by the worst evils of urban multi-deprivation. Disease, poverty, crime, social unrest — none of these were strangers to Limehouse, and its worst enclave was almost certainly the area immediately surrounding the Canal and Basin that feature in this novel.

The Regents Canal was built in the early nineteenth century in order to link the Grand Junction Canal at Paddington with the Thames, using barges that could convey goods back and forth from the ocean-going vessels coming up the Thames to be unloaded at Regents Canal Docks, better known today as 'Limehouse Basin'. In keeping with the etymology of the time the Canal was known as the 'Limehouse Cut', and like other waterways of its type it rapidly became a depository for everyone's unwanted items, including, on occasions, dead bodies. It was therefore hardly surprising that it also became a breeding ground for pestilence of all descriptions. Chief among these was cholera.

The history of cholera outbreaks in Victorian London is coterminous with the efforts of those in authority to 'do something' about human sewage, a natural breeding medium for a disease that first came to London on board ships from the Bay of Bengal, and devastated the city three times during the nineteenth century. As described in the pages you have read, the work of dedicated engineers led to the creation of a sewer network for the wealthier parts of London, but it would be a long time before Limehouse found its way to the head of the construction queue.

It was regarded as a 'no go' area even by battle-hardened 'bobbies' employed by the Metropolitan Police, and was hardly a suitable candidate for social or medical reform experiments. The 'Fenian Barracks' are also taken from history, in which large numbers of resentful Irish immigrants lived in defiance of the authorities, frequently barricading the streets against them, and fomenting civil unrest at every opportunity, including their support for the 'Match Girls Strike' that took place in 1888, only a few years before the one in which this novel is set.

This was made much easier by the existence of 'Rookeries' — densely constructed terraces of slum tenements that housed thousands of occupants in various degrees of squalor, deprivation and criminality. I did not invent the creation of 'galleries' between upper floors, through which those sought by the authorities could make their escape, a practice still in existence in Glasgow suburbs in the 1970s. Nor was the idea of defrauding the authorities by claiming to establish and maintain an orphanage an invention of mine, and it was exposed in a contemporary issue of the investigative journal of the day, *Truth*.

So surely 'Spring Heeled Jack' leapt out of my fertile imagination? If so, then contemporary accounts of this terrifying urban myth were also inventions. He was responsible for more than one overheated newspaper article in the period from 1837 until his last alleged appearance in 1904, and was no doubt used as a 'bogey man' threat by parents seeking to discipline their children.

I was able to borrow other snippets from recorded history. For example, the account early in the novel of a fictitious nobleman conning impoverished ladies out of their jewellery was a direct reference to the case history of the unfortunate Adolf Beck, wrongly identified by some fifteen women as the man responsible for a series of frauds actually committed by one John Smith, for whom Beck served seven years until the injustice came to light. The Beck case occurred only two years after the date of this novel.

So could human triangles be formed in order to effect entry to a room high in a building? The Perricone brothers of Van Nuys, California, proved that it can be done when, in November 1941, they employed their former vaudeville act in order to access a balcony and murder the hoodlum who had put their younger sister in hospital.

And of course I didn't invent Florence Nightingale. In fact one could say that she invented herself, becoming a living legend in nursing following her pioneering work in Scutari during the Crimean War. She was, by 1894, into her thirty-fourth year training nurses in St Thomas's Hospital, and she becomes a worthy mentor for the redoubtable Adelaide West in the next novel in the series, *Death Among the Nightingales.*

I would welcome any feedback and support that you, the reader, can supply. You can, of course, write a review on **Amazon** or **Goodreads** or you can contact me online via my Facebook page: **DavidFieldAuthor**. I'm more than happy to respond to observations, reviews, questions, or anything else that occurs to you, or to join in any 'thread' that you care to begin.

I look forward to getting to know you better online.

David

davidfieldauthor.com

SAPERE
BOOKS

Printed in Great Britain
by Amazon

81226717R00122